BONE SHOP

BONE SHOP

T.A. PRATT

The Merry Blacksmith Press

2012

Bone Shop

Cover art by Dan Dos Santos
www.dandossantos.com

For information, address:

The Merry Blacksmith Press
70 Lenox Ave.
West Warwick, RI 02893

merryblacksmith.com

Published in the USA by The Merry Blacksmith Press

ISBN—0-61567-563-8
978-0-61567-563-3

DEDICATION

This one is for all the readers who supported the experiment.

I very literally could not have done it without you.

Chapter One

MARLA MASON spent the afternoon of her sixteenth birthday with a pyromaniac named Jenny Click. They sat shoulder-to-shoulder against the support pillar of an overpass, trying to stay out of the late spring rain, and discussed their options.

"The thing is, maybe I should follow my passion," Jenny said. She wore a transparent raincoat over an increasingly ratty sweater and a rapidly-disintegrating pair of jeans.

"Which passion?" Marla said. "Sex, drugs, or setting fires?" They hadn't known one another very long, but spending time together on the street helped you learn a lot about the essentials of a person.

"Well, any of them," Jenny said, scratching her long nose absently. She had thin blonde hair, big blue eyes, lots of little burn scars on her hands, and a general air of jittery craziness that made Marla feel calm and grounded by comparison. "But being a hooker means getting a pimp, or getting beat up, and even with a pimp you get beat up half the time anyway, I hear. Still, it's an option."

Marla made a noncommittal grunting sound. She'd run away from her home back in Indiana for a lot of reasons, but one of them was the way her mother's drunken boyfriends—or one-night-stand bar pickups—had leered and grabbed and groped at her. She wasn't going to submit to such things, and worse, now that she was on her own. Which did limit her options, admittedly.

"Or drugs, there aren't a lot of girl dealers, but maybe that's, like, a market I could exploit?" Jenny fished a cigarette from a cavernous pocket and lit it with her nicest possession, a Zippo she'd stolen from her dad, inscribed with the initials "JWC"—her dad's initials, and close enough, she said, to hers. She spun up the fire and stared at the flame for a long

1

moment, eyes intense with concentration, until Marla snapped her fingers.

Jenny blinked, lit her cigarette, inhaled, snapped shut the lighter, and nodded. "Right. Sorry. But I mean maybe girls would be more comfortable buying whatever from another girl?"

"I don't know if any of the gangs would, uh, hire you. And even if you knew a dealer you could buy from, you'd need money to get started." Privately, Marla figured Jenny would consume any drugs she acquired before she could sell them—as far as Marla knew Jenny would try *anything*—and that would just end up getting her killed, or turned out, or something otherwise bad.

"Okay, so that leaves fire. My dad always said 'find what you love and do it for life,' but he sold fucking insurance, so who was he fooling? Maybe I could get a job as an arsonist. You know, burn places down for insurance money? I could join the... mob or whatever. I mean, I set fires *anyway*. Might as well get paid for it."

Marla liked hanging out with Jenny because she had a reputation as an utter lunatic—she'd once torched an unattended mail truck, the story went, because she wanted a fire to keep her warm—and people tended to give her, and anyone she was with, a wide berth. Marla could fight a little, her brother had taught her some dirty tricks, but it was smarter and easier to avoid conflict altogether, so that was the advantage of hanging out with Jenny.

The disadvantage was having to listen to the ridiculous crap that came out of her mouth.

"The problem, as I see it," Marla said carefully, "is that, if you set a fire for the insurance money, you'd probably want to stand there and watch it burn, maybe even until the cops got there."

Jenny waved her cigarette dismissively, and Marla leaned back to avoid being scorched. "I can work around it. Fires always attract a crowd. I can just... melt into the crowd. Nah, it'll work. It's good. Having a plan is good."

"Not sure how you get into a business like that," Marla said.

"There's a bar, on the other side of the river near the east bridge, I hear there's a guy there. Like a crime boss guy. Heard my dealer talking to *his* dealer about it, he's the guy they buy from, supposed to be a big deal. Maybe I'll go down there and, sort of, apply for a job?"

"Just go up to him and say, 'Hi, I like to start fires, you have any openings?'" Marla shook her head. "Best case, you get laughed at. Worst case, they call the cops."

Jenny tossed her cigarette aside, and was quiet for a long moment. "Your problem, Marla," she said at last, "is you just find excuses to tear stuff down instead of actually *doing* anything." Jenny rose and walked off into the rain.

"Is *that* my problem," Marla said, to the empty air. "I've been wondering."

Maybe it was a problem. Maybe she should do something about it.

After spending several months in Felport, Marla didn't quite have a comfortable routine, but she had a series of strategies that covered her basic necessities. There were a few places she could sleep safely, though fewer than there had been in spring and summer—competition for relatively dry indoor places got fierce as the temperatures dropped along with the leaves from the trees.

Her days were spent mostly in the big public library downtown, reading whatever caught her eye—American history, Sun Tzu, mystery novels, popular science, first-person accounts of bear attacks, mythology, memoirs from formerly homeless and drug-addicted people, some of them even genuine.

For food she mostly dumpster-dived, having met some enterprising freegans her first month in town, who'd shown her the prime places to scavenge. She'd also learned a few hustles from her brother, who was the prince of the small-town con men, but most of them were no good to her—it was hard to find people to play cards with a teenage girl, and a lot of the better scams required confederates or access to bars, two things it was tricky for her to acquire. Jenny had been too unreliable for such work, and once she vanished to pursue her career as an arsonist, Marla made it a point not to get close to anyone else. She had to learn to live on her own. Still, she knew enough short cons to keep her in pocket money, and she could use her youth and female-ness to her advantage, since people didn't expect to get ripped off by someone like her.

Living outside or in squats made you stinky and disreputable, though, and that *was* a problem, and pretty quickly. Back home maybe she'd be able to steal clothes off the line in somebody's back yard, but things were different in the city. Shoplifting new clothes was no good, because she soon looked ratty enough that store security started following her as soon as she walked in the door.

But then, in early summer, she made a life-changing score.

Marla was hanging out in a little park in an upscale neighborhood north of the river, sitting on a picnic table watching some people do tai-chi and wondering if the slow deliberate movements could translate into actual ass-kicking. It must have been a genuinely *martial* martial art at some point, right?

A young, blonde mother pushing a stroller and talking on a cell phone parked her baby carriage at the table next to Marla's. Marla glanced over to see if she had anything worth stealing—distracted moms in parks sometimes wandered away from their possessions, though usually when chasing toddlers, and this kid was both younger than that and asleep. Nothing caught her eye, but the mother started digging through an over-stuffed diaper bag that apparently doubled as a purse, trying to pull out a hardcover Danielle Steele novel while continuing her phone conversation—a stream of invective aimed at the baby's father and, by extension, all men everywhere.

She liberated the book, but knocked over the bag in the process, and a rain of lipstick tubes and tattered receipts and pacifiers and her wallet and its contents pattered onto the ground.

Just then the baby started screaming, and the mother simply froze, phone in one hand, book in the other, apparently overwhelmed by the sensory assault.

Ever one to turn another's distraction to her advantage, Marla said, "Let me help you with that," and began picking up the make-up and baby accoutrements from the ground.

"Oh, thank you," the mom said, still distracted, and bent to tend to the wailing baby, clucking and cooing and making nonsense soothing noises.

Marla was hoping to find a wad of cash—credit cards weren't much good to her, everyone wanted to see ID, because Marla was so grungy—but beyond a few loose coins, there was no money in the mess. A library card, a Triple-A card, a car insurance card, useless, useless—but when she saw the white-and-red YMCA card, she palmed it and slipped it in her pocket, just in case. "Here you go," Marla said, putting the last of the dropped items in the diaper bag, and the mother nodded and mumbled more thanks while picking up the baby. She didn't notice the theft, and had never even looked at Marla's face.

Marla sauntered off around a corner. She'd walked past the uptown Y a few times, and it wasn't too far. If the people at the desk were attentive she'd never get in, but maybe…

She walked half a dozen blocks, then went up the steps and through the automatic doors. The Y was pretty pleasant, clean and bustling even at midday, and the lobby smelled faintly of chlorine from the pool downstairs. The people at the desk looked promisingly bored. Marla pretended to read the big row of plaques on the wall honoring various donors while she watched people go in and out. The setup was better than she'd hoped.

Nobody bothered to look at your ID, you just held up the card to the little electric eye by the turnstile and pushed on through. Since you didn't have to use the card to get *out*, she'd be fine even if the card's rightful owner went in while Marla was there. Distracted-mommy could get a replacement card—it would be an inconvenience, sure, but this barely qualified as a crime by Marla's standards. As long as mommy kept her membership, Marla should be able to come as often as she liked. She owned a pair of shorts and a grimy t-shirt that would pass as gym clothes until she could acquire something better.

The Y became her second home, a paradise she visited daily, even though it was a few miles from her preferred squat. The place was worth the walk, though—once inside, she could shower, swim, use the exercise machines, sit in the sauna, use the hot tub, even take a bunch of classes for free, not that she did; the appeal of being yelled at by a woman in a leotard escaped her.

She was often tempted to break into lockers to see what she could find, but it would mean trouble if she were caught. She did snatch the occasional unattended deodorant, bottle of lotion, or other useful little things.

With regular access to a shower—and after stealing a perfectly nice sundress off a rack during one of the summer sidewalk sales, running like hell from a persistent saleswoman who pursued her for blocks, despite the disadvantage of her high heels—Marla was in business. She could get cleaned up and go to any store in the mall and take whatever she could fit in her bag and her pockets. She had a great sense for when the store detectives were taking a special interest in her—acquired during all those years of watchfulness at home—and she never got caught, though she had some close moments. Between the stuff she could pawn and the stuff she could wear, autumn was shaping up nicely, despite the drafty walls in the abandoned building where she was living.

Marla was in the process of stealing some new underwear from a swanky lingerie store when she next saw Jenny Click.

Jenny looked… *good.* Almost unrecognizably so. She was dressed in a decidedly non-ratty chocolate-brown sweater, tight white jeans, and a white denim jacket. Her hair was teased and hairsprayed, her make-up somehow simultaneously complex and discreet, and she was less thin and strung-out looking—though still a long way from fat. Moreover, the way she walked was totally different, without the tightly-wound watchfulness that took in every possible threat from every possible direction. She had the kind of pleased, faraway look that she usually only got from looking at fire.

Jenny had clearly passed into some other world, and Marla was instantly suspicious, and jealous, and resentful, and felt comparatively filthy and ill-fed; her instinct was to withdraw and slink away.

But she was also curious. That was, perhaps, her dominant trait. So she said, as nonchalantly as she could, "Hi, Jenny."

Jenny turned her head, saw Marla, and smiled widely. She glided over and embraced her and clasped Marla's hands in her own and made effusive noises. Marla noticed that Jenny's fingers weren't burn-scarred anymore; how had *that* happened? Could you get plastic surgery on your hands?

"Come, let me buy you something to eat," Jenny said, and Marla allowed herself to be led to the food court, the usual multi-ethnic array of fried rice and pizza and hamburgers and breaded chicken, all fundamentally tasting like cardboard. Marla bought as much as she could carry—she usually only got this food once it was cold and discarded—and sat down with a tottering pile of french fries and burgers and disgusting little hot apple pies that tasted like pastry filled with sweet glue; but they were filling.

Jenny had a salad. Which meant her concern was worrying about her weight instead of maximizing caloric intake. Which seemed, Marla realized, practically the mindset of an alien creature at this point. To have that kind of luxury, that kind of unconcern… *However she got where she is,* Marla thought, *I'm going to get there too.*

"Marla," Jenny said. "Are you still living… like we used to?"

"Living by my wits," Marla said, having encountered the phrase recently at the library and enjoying the opportunity to use it.

"I can help you. I think. If you want."

"Charity is always appreciated. Cash only, though, I can't take credit cards."

Jenny laughed and shook her head. "I could help you that way, but it's better if I help you help yourself. My—a friend of mine taught me that. How would you like a job?"

"Doing what?"

"Waitressing. Probably. To start. But there's room for advancement."

Marla snorted around a mouthful of french fries. After swallowing, she said, "I've never waited tables. Who's going to hire me? I don't even have a phone or a home address. I can't even fill out an application."

"Just go down to the Bau Bau Room," Jenny said, writing down an address—with an eyebrow pencil!—on a napkin. "Go to the bar and ask for Rollo. Tell him I sent you." She grinned—a very uncharacteristic look for Jenny. Though maybe not for *this* Jenny. "Just go easy on him. You know you can overwhelm people when you really turn on the charm."

"That's always been a problem for me." Marla picked up the napkin. "I guess I'll give it a try. Is the money good? I mean, is this what you do?"

"It's what I started out doing," Jenny said. "Now I do… other things."

Marla wrinkled her nose. "You're not hooking, are you? If this guy Rollo's your pimp, I'm not interested."

"It's not like that." She stood up, slinging her stylish purse over her arm. "Though, when you get there… well. Just remember. It's not hooking. I *swear*."

"Ohh-kay. Hey, before you go. What happened to your hands? They used to be all scarred up, now they're not." Marla had heard of tact, subtlety, and decorum, but had seldom seen the point in using them.

Jenny held out her hands, palms facing away from her, as if examining her manicure. "Like I said. I learned to help myself. Go see Rollo. Maybe you'll learn something too." She waved and strolled into the depths of the mall.

Marla pocketed the napkin with the address. Then she ate the rest of her food. Then she ate the remains of Jenny's salad.

Then she went and shoplifted some underwear, because regardless of what tomorrow might bring, she still needed to look after today.

Chapter Two

THE BAU BAU ROOM was in an unlovely part of downtown, near a lot of check-cashing places and liquor stores and greasy pizza joints and a few weird remnants of Felport's rusty industrial past: a machine shop, a small-engine repair company, and a place that sold chemicals.

Marla found the ugliness comforting and familiar. With a name like The Bau Bau Room she hadn't exactly expected something swanky, but she'd worried.

The club occupied one bottom corner of a squat three-story building with offices above, mostly for the kind of lawyer who advertises on late night TV, though there was also a private detective, which Marla found sort of interesting. She'd only read about such people, never met one, though she suspected reality would diverge from fiction pretty swiftly if she ever did.

It was only about noon, but the front door of the place was unlocked, so she pushed her way in.

The Bau Bau Room owed a lot to red velvet. Red velvet walls, red velvet booths, even ratty red velvet on the bar stools, worn through in places by years of prolonged ass-contact. There were a few booths against the walls and lots of small round tables crowded around the clear focal point of the room: a hexagonal stage with mirrors on the wall behind it and a vertical metal pole in the center. Marla had never been inside a strip club before, but she knew one when she saw it, even sans strippers.

She hesitated, almost walked away, then thought of Jenny, all clean and together and unscarred, and went toward the bar.

A middle-aged bald guy with a bushy mustache and a diamond earring leaned on the bar flipping through a newspaper. "We're not open yet," he said, then glanced up at her. "And you're too young to drink anyway. Beat it." He went back to his paper.

Marla sat on the stool in front of him. "Are you Rollo?"

He looked up from the paper again, this time more carefully. "You don't look like a process server, but to be on the safe side, who wants to know?"

"Jenny sent me."

"Who the fuck is Jenny?"

That was not encouraging. "Jenny Click. Blonde, kind of skinny, long nose"—was that unkind?—"she said she got a job here a while—"

"Right, firebug Jenny, sure." He looked at Marla more closely, then shook his head. "Shit. How old are you?"

"Eighteen," Marla said promptly. Only a lie by 18 months or so. And she knew she could pass for older if called upon.

Rollo wasn't buying it though. He shook his head. "You got ID?"

"Not with me."

"Not anywhere, more like it, or if you do it's a lousy fake. But if you're friends with Jenny, you probably can't afford a fake ID. That kind of stuff's for the rich north side kids, or the suburban ones. But, okay, maybe we can work something out. You want to work here?"

"If the money's right."

He snorted. "A waitress job, you get about half of minimum wage and whatever tips you can hustle. You can make more dancing, but we're full up right now."

Marla shook her head. "That's fine. I'm not much of a dancer."

"It's more, you know, *undulating* than actual dancing, but anyway. Okay, waitress it is, if you qualify. Let's see 'em."

Marla frowned. "See what?"

"Your tits, hon. You can learn how to carry a tray full of drinks and make change, but good tits can't be taught."

Marla nodded thoughtfully. "So the waitresses are topless, too."

"The dancers are *more* than topless, eventually, but, yes."

Rollo didn't seem particularly interested in leering at her. He seemed to mostly wish she would go away. "No touching, right?"

"What, from me, or the customers? From me, no. From the customers, no, not in theory. Sometimes somebody might get grabby, you just catch the bouncer's eye and we toss him out. Maybe you think you can make like a *private* arrangement with a customer, but the management frowns on that kind of freelancing. Now show 'em or go apply for a job at McDonald's, would you?"

There was a perverse pleasure in the thought of taking money from drunken assholes—she assumed that would describe the clientele, imagining a roomful of men like her mother's innumerable boyfriends—and knowing a bouncer would toss them out if they dared to touch her.

Marla lifted up her shirt.

Rollo squinted, nodded, and said, "All right, you'd get better tips if they were bigger, but you're, what, sixteen, seventeen? Nobody's exactly gonna complain. And you're not so skinny I can see your skeleton, which was the main thing I worried about. We made Jenny go eat cheeseburgers and milkshakes for a week and come back when we couldn't count her ribs anymore."

"So I'm hired?"

"Come into the back room for a minute, and you will be."

"I'm not fucking you," Marla said.

"That's for sure. I prefer sleeping with women old enough to know their way around a little. Come on." He came around the bar and led her to an unmarked door near the back wall, then led her into the backstage area, where there were chipped vanity mirrors, cardboard boxes full of high heels and feather boas and miscellaneous bits of underwear, and a row of gray lockers. Beyond that was another door, with a cardboard sign reading "Office" tacked into the center. The room beyond was surprisingly spacious, furnished with dented filing cabinets and a big desk covered in paper clutter.

Rollo opened a closet and took out a camera on a tripod, then tacked a dark blue cloth up on the wall.

"Oh," Marla said. "You're making me a fake ID."

"Gotta have ID on file for you, and since you don't have your own…" He shrugged. "The cops don't bother us much, but every once in a while somebody comes down and wants to see our records."

"I can't pay for this," Marla said.

"So no money up front, and we'll take it out of your earnings, all right? And you'll be able to buy your own booze afterward."

Marla didn't drink much. She could rarely afford to have her faculties blurred. "How much will it cost?"

Rollo shook his head. "You are one cautious kid. Tell you what, we'll call it half the tips you make tonight, okay?"

Marla nodded. She was having a hard time seeing how one went from serving drinks topless to being detoxed and scar-free and apparently happy like Jenny was, but this didn't seem the time to ask.

She stood for the camera, trying to "Look bored like you're at the DMV" as Rollo suggested. He took down her name and birthdate—"We'll just change the year"—and height and weight, and made her fill out some employment forms "Come back at 7, I'll get this laminated for you, and one of the other waitresses will show you the ropes. Not literally the ropes. It's not that kind of club. Don't fuck up tonight and you can come back tomorrow. Okay?"

"Sure," Marla said. Then, after a moment's thought: "Thanks."

"Thank Jenny," Rollo said. "You hadn't dropped her name, I'd have kicked you out the door on your ass."

Having a job, and being expected to show up somewhere at a certain time, was a novelty, but the structure wasn't entirely unpleasant. The uniform—which consisted of rather tight shorts, a little apron, and nothing else—initially made her uncomfortable, but after a few hours the first night she hardly noticed her own nudity. She had little in common with the other waitresses, and didn't spend much time talking to them, but she shared their universal dislike for the dancers, who looked down on the waitresses as inferior beings.

Nobody ever mentioned Jenny, and Marla didn't bring her up, either.

The clientele was as boorish as she'd expected. At first she made an effort to smile at them, but soon realized that the few men (and occasional women) who paid attention to her at all didn't look much higher than her chest anyway, so she allowed herself to be impassive or scowl as much as necessary.

The tips were pretty good, though, at least on weekends. At the end of her first week, when it was clear she wasn't a drunk, a thief (at least in this context), or a drug addict, Rollo got her a room in a run-down apartment nearby, the kind of place with one shared bathroom per floor and a hotplate on a table for a kitchen. But it came with a bed and a dresser and it was *hers*.

Customers occasionally swatted her ass as she went by, and she learned, to her annoyance, that the bouncer was unwilling to throw them out for that, though he'd warn them to keep their hands to themselves. Marla consoled herself by wishing horrible deaths upon them, but resisted the urge to assault anyone.

Until one Saturday night, after about a month working at the bar, the best man at a bachelor party full of merry twentysomethings grabbed her as she was going by, knocking the tray from her hands as he pulled her into his lap. He reached around with both hands to grab her breasts, laughing raucously in her ear, and even though Marla saw the bouncer coming her way, she didn't wait.

Marla stomped his instep with her heel, threw her head back—he gasped, and she felt his nose crunch—and seized his hands, twisting his thumbs back as hard as she could as she stood up. "No touching," she said, and half the club applauded while the other half, including the rest of the bachelor party, gaped.

"You bitch," the best man said, clutching his bloody nose, "I'll beat the shit out of you—"

The bouncer put a big hand on the man's shoulder, and said, gently, "You want her to hurt you *worse*? Time to go, pal." He hustled the whole group out of the bar, and Marla smoothed down her hair and squatted to pick up her tray—she didn't feel like bending over and giving the room a nice look at her ass.

When she stood up, a fat guy with a comb-over and a cigar in his fingers beckoned to her. "Come here, would you?"

Marla had seen him before a few times, drinking Scotch and watching the dancers and not causing any fuss, but she'd never waited on him, and didn't have a good sense of whether he was an asshole or not. "Why, you want some of what that guy got?"

He was a red-faced guy, and his face got redder when he laughed. "Nah, just come here, sit down."

Marla shook her head. "My boss won't like—"

"Kid, *I'm* your boss. I'm Artie Mann. This is my joint."

"Oh," Marla said. "Am I fired? For hitting that guy?"

"Don't make it a habit, but no, you're not fired. You had some cause. Sit and talk to me." Marla joined him, secretly happy to be off her feet for a little while. Artie stared fixedly at her breasts while he spoke, which didn't do much to endear him to her. "How long you been working here?"

"A few weeks."

"What made you come into this place?"

She shrugged. "My friend Jenny said you were hiring."

"Jenny. Jenny Click?"

"Yeah. She used to work here?"

Artie nodded.

"But now she's… moved up in the organization?" Marla figured this had to be the crime boss, the guy Jenny wanted to meet.

"Sure," Artie said. "You're a friend of hers, huh?" He looked at her speculatively. "You seemed to know what you were doing, cracking that guy's nose, stomping his foot, like that. Somebody teach you?"

"There was a guy who used to hassle me, back home, so my brother showed me a few things, to take care of myself." That guy had hassled her one too many times, and things had gotten out of hand, and now he wouldn't ever hassle her or anyone else again—but that wasn't something she wanted to talk about, or even think about.

"Pretty tough, kid. What's your name?"

"Marla."

"I think Jenny mighta mentioned you. When's your next night off?"

"Tomorrow," she said.

"Listen. You want to come over to my house, maybe have some dinner, and see Jenny?"

Marla's resisted the urge to sigh. So that was the explanation. Jenny hadn't "moved up in the organization"—she'd just moved in with the boss, who had doubtless paid for her hair, her clothes, and to clean up her scarred hands. And, what, now he wanted Marla to join his harem or something? "I don't know…"

"Don't say no to the boss," he said, mock-sternly.

"I guess it'd be good to see Jenny again." If he tried anything on her, she could just walk away. And if he didn't want her to walk away, she could persuade him. Breaking two noses in two days would be a new record for her.

"It's a deal," he said. "Come over here around six, I'll have a car waiting. Now go earn some money."

When the club closed, Marla nodded her farewells and went out into the street. It wasn't the best neighborhood, but her apartment was only a block and a half away, and Rollo had assured her that the local thugs knew better than to mess with any of the Bau Bau Room's girls—Artie Mann had juice around here, apparently. Though she saw the occasional shadowy figure lurking in a doorway, she'd never been bothered.

Until now. The best man who'd pulled her into his lap earlier stepped out of an alley just a few doors away from her place. He had cotton wadding sticking out of his nostrils—his friends must have taken him to the emergency room to get his broken nose patched up. He looked ridiculous, but he also looked pissed-off, and three of his friends were lurking behind him, shadowed by the old brick buildings that lined the street.

"Thought I'd let you get away with hitting me, bitch?" the best man said, voice thick and mushy from his blocked-up nose and, probably, booze. "Nobody fucks with me. How about we drag you back here and see how tough you are?"

Marla glanced around, knowing it was futile—this late the street was deserted, and her neighbors weren't the sort who'd come to the aid of a screaming woman. Which meant her options were limited. But that didn't mean she had no options.

She took her keys from her pocket and grasped the longest one firmly between her thumb and fingers. It wasn't much of a weapon, but it was better than fingernails. Maybe she should start carrying a knife. As calmly as she could, she said, "There are four of you, and one of me. That means I probably can't stop you."

"Damn right you can't—" the best man began, but Marla shook her head sharply.

"Shut up," she said, because it was worth a try. Amazingly, he did, though probably not for long, so she went on while she had the floor. "I can't stop you. But I can make it cost you. If I can gouge out your eyes, I will. If I can bite off an ear, or a nose, or something more tender, I will. I'll fight as hard and as long as I can, and whenever I can, I'll make sure to hurt you where it shows. You'll have some ugly marks on your faces to explain at that wedding you're all going to."

"Come on, man, maybe we should go," said one of the lurkers. None of them seemed particularly happy about this situation, judging by their body language. Marla began to see a glimmer of hope of getting out of this unhurt. If she could do something sufficiently nasty to the best man, fast enough, the others would probably just melt away.

"No way," the best man said. "She can't weigh more than a hundred, hundred and ten pounds. Couple of you grab her arms and she won't be able to do shit."

"You sound like you've done this before," Marla said. "You make a habit of jumping girls alone in the street? Probably the only way you get any action at all, right?" Maybe taunting him was a bad idea, but she was tired, and pissed off, and he was some idiot from the suburbs who thought he was a big man. She wanted to tell him how small he was, and make sure his friends heard it, too.

"That's it, you're fucked now," the best man said, and came toward her, two of his companions moving away from the wall to join him, while the one who'd acted as the voice of restraint just stood there shaking his head. Three against one wasn't much better odds than four against one, unfortunately. She'd promised to make this cost them, and she would.... but she didn't want to think about what it would cost *her*.

"No touching the girls without their permission," said Artie Mann strolling out of—where, exactly? The middle of the street? But she hadn't *seen* him there. He wore the same untucked Hawaiian shirt, and had perhaps the same fat cigar in his mouth. "That rule applies inside and outside the club."

"Get lost," the best man said, still staring at Marla. "This doesn't have shit to do with you."

"Okay," Artie said, and sucked on his cigar, making the end glow redly. Then he flicked the ashes toward the best man—

—and the ash somehow swelled into a fist-sized fireball that struck him in the chest, knocking him down. His friends jumped back, and the best man screamed, beating at his shirt, which was singed and smoking. The men all looked at Artie, who took another long pull on his cigar, and exhaled a cloud of smoke.... and kept exhaling, smoke thick as fog, great rolling gouts of it, and when the smoke touched them, the men dropped to their knees, gagging.

Artie walked over to Marla, put his hand on her shoulder, and said, "I'll walk you home, kid."

"What did you do?" Marla said as they walked wide into the street to skirt around the choking cloud and the men inside.

"Nothing permanent. Mostly just scared 'em."

"But *how*?"

"What'd it look like?"

"It *looked* like magic," Marla said. "But I want to know what it *was*."

"You got it in one. Magic."

Marla shook her head. "You have a magical cigar?"

"No. I have magic, and I also have a cigar."

"I don't believe in magic," Marla said, though the statement was slightly less true than it had been two minutes ago.

Artie sighed. "Come on, kid. Skepticism might take you farther than faith, but you won't have nearly as much fun getting there. We'll talk about it more when you come over tomorrow." They reached her building and went up the steps, and Marla, who still had her key clutched defensively in her hand, unlocked the door. She wasn't sure what was happening, but she was very interested in finding out.

She had one thing to say, though: "I didn't need your help. I can take care of myself."

Marla was afraid he'd laugh, or argue, but he just nodded seriously, cigar bobbing in his mouth. "I believe it. But you shouldn't have to do it all yourself. You work for me. That includes a certain protection. Besides, our situations were reversed, you'd do the same for me."

Marla shook her head. "I can't do… things like that."

"Don't worry about it," Artie said. "You're young yet." And he sauntered off into the night.

Chapter Three

MARLA BOUGHT A KNIFE in a pawn shop, a short blade sharp on both edges with a bone handle and a worn brown leather sheath. The knife felt good in her hand, light and fast, even though she didn't know much about knives; her brother had never taught her to use one, and no one else had ever taught her much of anything.

It would make a better weapon than her door key, though, if the time came, and she slipped it into the pocket of her jeans before going to the club to wait for Artie Mann's car.

She got there a little early and pushed through the door into the familiar dimness. There wasn't much of a crowd yet—the after-work slumming yuppies were still stuck in traffic on the bridges, coming from the more prosperous north side—and Vanessa, the milk-skinned redhead with the coke problem, was absentmindedly ambling around the stripper pole in a red g-string.

Rollo was behind the bar, and Marla slipped onto a stool to wait. He sidled over. "What'll it be—oh. Didn't recognize you with your shirt on." He grinned nastily, but that was his way of being friendly, and Marla just sniffed.

"I bet you don't even know what color my eyes are," she said.

"You've got eyes?" He leaned forward, put his elbows on the bar, and cupped his chin in his hands. "I hear you're going over to the boss's house."

Marla nodded. "Should I be worried?"

Rollo laughed. "After your performance in here last night, he probably wants to hire you as enforcer, go to work for a loan shark breaking people's legs. Nah, I wouldn't worry. Artie's all right. He's got the manners of an ape-man, but he's a straight shooter." Rollo belched, as if to underscore his own lack of manners.

"How much do you know about his business?"

Rollo shook his head. "I just work here. I hear things, but who knows? He owns some bars, couple of adult bookstores, the last porno theater in the city, and some dry cleaners, too, if you believe that. Maybe he's into other stuff. I don't ask, he doesn't tell me." He glanced around. "Though he did set me up with the laminating machine and such in the back. So he's got a pretty broad definition of legitimate business."

The door swung open, and a broad-shouldered Hispanic man in a dirty-looking tuxedo and a chauffeur's cap stepped in. "Rollo, how's it going," he said.

"No complaints, Ernesto. You driving tonight?"

Ernesto pointed at his head. "I'm wearing this stupid fucking hat, ain't I? You Marla?"

She nodded.

"Great, come on, the car's waiting." He beckoned, and Marla slid off the stool, nodding farewell to Rollo. They went into the evening, and Marla stopped on the sidewalk to stare at the long, low, sleek black car parked by a fire hydrant. Ernesto grinned at her. "Nice, huh? It's a Bentley."

Marla had never much given a crap about cars—she preferred to walk everywhere, that's how you got to know a place—but it was a beautiful machine, and she just nodded. Ernesto went around to the driver's side and got in, and Marla hesitated. Was she supposed to get in the back seat, or what? Ernesto leaned over and shoved open the front passenger door, answering the question for her, and she slid inside.

"I'm not a chauffeur, usually," he said, driving along the narrow, trash-littered streets. "I drive Artie around sometimes, do other stuff for him. He gave me this stupid fucking hat as a joke, and I wear it every time I drive, so he knows I can *take* a joke. See?

Marla nodded, wondering if this was supposed to be some kind of advice.

"I've got some errands to run for Artie tonight, so I won't be around, but you know Jenny, right? So there'll be a familiar face."

Marla shook her head, annoyed as always by circumspection, by people leaving things out. "What's the point of all this? Why does Artie want to see me? I work for him, and maybe I owe him because he helped me out last night, but what am I walking into here?"

Ernesto drove without saying anything for a while, out of the bad neighborhood toward one of the bridges that spanned the Balsamo River. Apparently Artie lived in a nicer neighborhood than the one where he kept his businesses. Well, who could blame him?

Finally Ernesto said, "I used to be just some guy. Good with cars, did some work for my uncle at his body shop. Then I met Artie. Got into a scrape, he helped me out of it. Saw something in me. Now, without going into too many details… I'm more than just some guy. Maybe Artie sees something in you, too. I don't know what his plans are for you, exactly. But keep an open mind. Hear him out."

Marla shrugged. "Not like I've got anything better going on. My job now is, I carry drinks with my boobs on display."

"I'm sure you're wonderful at it."

"So. Magic. I'm supposed to believe in that now?" Marla had spent the night staring at the ceiling, considering that question. She'd known people back home who believed in ghosts, who claimed to have seen them. She had a cousin who had fits and said she saw angels sometimes during her seizures. Marla herself had never experienced anything especially uncanny—her life had been pretty banal, with the banality sometimes shading into evil—until last night. She'd seen something, certainly. Special effects? A trick? A con? But why con her? She didn't have anything worth stealing.

"I don't know what you should believe," Ernesto said. "I wouldn't presume to tell you. But if you see something, do you trust your senses, or not? Do you assume you're going crazy, or assume the world is crazier than you ever knew? I guess that's the decision you have to make."

"What about you?" Ernesto seemed down-to-earth, grounded, *ordinary*. For that matter, Artie was a fat guy with a comb-over. If there was real magic, would it be so unglamorous? Or was the ordinariness just a way of hiding the magic? "You do magic too?"

"I do whatever Artie needs me to," Ernesto said. Then he turned the radio to some station with people yelling in Spanish and started chuckling, which was as clear an attempt to end conversation as Marla had ever seen.

She was annoyed by her own monolinguality. She wanted to know what was so funny on the radio. She'd have to learn Spanish. She'd have to learn *everything*.

After leaving the city and winding up along the coast road for a few minutes, Ernesto turned down a long paved driveway toward a black iron gate, which opened apparently by magic before them, and closed after them when they passed. "Here we are," Ernesto said, and stopped the car in the turnaround drive near the front door.

Artie Mann's house didn't look like much, just one wide low story of timber and glass, the yard tastefully landscaped, and Marla grunted. "Thought it'd be bigger."

Ernesto grinned. "Artie's house is like an iceberg. This is just the tip. I'll go in with you." They went to the front door, which Ernesto opened without a key—must be a safe neighborhood, or could you even call it a neighbhorhood when the nearest house was miles away?

He opened the door and made a sweeping after-you gesture, so Marla stepped inside.

She'd expected a mansion, and Artie did live in a mansion, more or less, but her experience with such places was largely limited to movies and television, so she'd envisioned something with white pillars out front and a fountain in the middle of the driveway and servants in black-and-white lined up on the steps.

Instead Artie's house was a multi-story architectural lichen clinging to the hillside overlooking the ocean, complete with cantilevered decks on several floors. From the front door she could see across to the far wall, which was all glass, providing a spectacular view of the bay.

Ernesto led her across a sparsely-furnished living room bigger than Marla's apartment to a spiral staircase. "There's an elevator, but Artie said you should take the stairs. Down you go. Stop descending when you see some people." Ernesto patted her on the back companionably, then left by the front door.

She thought about taking the elevator, mostly out of contrariness, but decided maybe Artie was trying to see if she could follow instructions. Which she could, to a point.

Marla looked around the room. White carpet, a couch, a couple of chairs, some shelves holding vaguely erotic-looking bits of old statuary: round-bellied Venuses, intricately carved stone phalluses sitting upright and looking accusatory, and a hunk of rock painted with a petroglyph of a hunchbacked guy with dreadlocks or head-tentacles or something playing a flute. At least there weren't black velvet paintings of naked women. Artie's vulgarity was classy.

She went down the staircase, spiraling around into another room, this one paneled in dark wood and much larger, extending back into the hillside. There were a couple of leather armchairs, but most of the space was given over to reading material—the walls were covered in shelves, and there were tottering piles of magazines and books, with more heaped on library tables.

"Hello?" she said. "Jenny? Artie? Anybody?" She stepped off the staircase and went to the nearest shelf. Books by Anais Nin, Pauline Reage, the Marquis de Sade, and Leopold von Sacher-Masoch were mixed in with random back issues of *Hustler* and *Juggs* and other such sophisticated literary journals.

She went back to the staircase and down again, into what appeared to be a giant walk-in closet, a neatly-organized space full of hanging garments, the walls lined with shelves and drawers and full-length mirrors. Shoes of all sorts—from fuzzy green slippers to thigh-high vinyl boots to strange black leather things with tiny padlocks on the straps and absurd 8-inch heels—rested in pretty pairs on most of the horizontal surfaces.

Marla went to the half-shut door and pushed it open, revealing a hallway that burrowed deeper into the hill. There was the suggestion of light and voices at the end of the hall, so she stepped in, saying, "Hey, is anybody—"

She sensed movement behind her (back in the closet? How was that possible?), and without even thinking she slipped her knife from its sheath. A rough hand seized her shoulder—and, ow, something was *poking* her there, *stinging* her—and spun her around. She added her own momentum to the spin, bringing up her elbow to smash whoever had grabbed her. Her blow whiffed harmlessly—he'd dodged somehow—but Marla could see her attacker now, even though he was backlit by the light from the big windows overlooking the bay.

He wore a black bondage mask with a zippered mouth, and a strange green light emerged from the eye sockets and nostril holes, with no hint of an actual face inside—whatever this was, it wasn't human. Its body was clad in a leather catsuit, hands in claw-tipped leather gloves—they were *still* digging into her shoulder, fuck—and its whole body rippled and bulged weirdly.

Magic, a trick, whatever this was—it didn't matter. Only her actions mattered.

Marla tore free of its clawed grip and drove her knife into the center of its chest. The body provided no resistance, and Marla fell forward, off balance, her weight plunging the knife through the leather and into the wall beyond, pinning the leather apparition to the wood paneling. Its body rippled and twitched, then the green glow faded, and it slumped...

...nothing but a suit of clothes hanging against the wall on the point of her knife. The bondage mask fell to the floor, as did the wicked gloves.

"Well, that was disappointing."

Marla wrenched her knife from the wall and turned to the end of the hall, where a boy about her age—messy blond mass of hair, face of an angel, wicked curved smile—leaned in the now-open doorway.

"Oh, I dunno, Daniel," Artie said, patting the boy's shoulder as he squeezed by and came down the hall toward Marla, who did not lower her knife. "That was a pretty good act of violence, I'd say."

"But it was hardly *magic*," Daniel said.

Marla relaxed, slightly. "This was a test?"

"Yeah, sorry about that," Artie said. "But it wouldn't have been much good if we'd warned you beforehand. You planning on stabbing me?"

Marla looked at the knife in her hand, shrugged, and sheathed it. "Not just now."

"The startle reaction, having something jump out at you from behind and grab you, sometimes it makes interesting things happen."

"When we did that to Jenny, she made the poppet *explode*." Daniel's voice was somewhere halfway between reproach and admiration.

Marla filed the information away, and made a mental note not to startle Jenny. "So I failed the test? Because I didn't do something magic?"

"Nah," Artie said. "Jenny was an oddball case. Lots of pent-up potential. Most people, it doesn't go that way. But magic is about will." He poked the pile of leather with his foot. "Will, kid, is something you've got."

"Great." Marla rubbed her shoulder where the claws had pricked her.

"Fetish gloves," Artie said. "For kinky types who like a little pain with their pleasure, you know? Sensation play."

Marla wondered if that was the sort of thing Artie was into—it seemed likely, he had the stuff in his house—but she didn't particularly want to speculate about Artie's sex life. He was old, and built like a manatee. Daniel, on the other hand, was lovely to look at, and speculations in that direction happened automatically… even if he was trying too hard to look bored and above it all.

But what did she know? He was some kind of sorcerer or something. Maybe he was bored and above it all.

"Come on, sit down, we'll talk." Artie went past Daniel into the room beyond. Daniel arched one eyebrow at her—how long had he practiced *that* in the mirror, she wondered?—then turned and went through the doorway.

Nice butt, too.

The next room was refreshingly normal, a big overstuffed couch scattered with pages from newspapers, an enormous flat-screen TV hanging on the wall, armchairs and reading lamps; this was a place where people actually spent time and lived. Artie sat in a recliner and put his feet up, while Daniel lounged with practiced nonchalance on the couch. Marla sat at the far end away from him. "Where's Jenny?"

"Out running an errand," Artie said. "She'll be back in half an hour or so. If she's later than that we'll just eat without her. What're we having, anyway, Daniel?"

"Lobster thermidor. Coq au vin. Beef Wellington. Cherries jubilee—"

Artie snorted. "Come on, come on."

Daniel shrugged. "Some steaks under the broiler, I guess, baked potatoes, I'll open a can of green beans or something and heat it up. There's ice cream, I think, unless you ate it all."

"I don't suppose you know how to cook, Marla?" Artie said.

Marla shook her head. "Spaghetti with sauce out of a jar. Scrambled eggs. That's about it." Did he want to hire her to be a cook? Better than a hooker, though she wasn't particularly qualified for either position.

"Yeah, figures. Daniel's better than me and I'm better than Jenny, who burns everything—that's like a joke, I know, but also true—but none of us are worth a damn. Not a lot of places deliver this far out of the city, just pizza. Usually we fend for ourselves, eat whatever wherever. But, hey, you're our guest, so for you, we cook."

"You usually sic—what did you call it? A poppet?—on your guests?"

"Little test, that's all, like I said." Artie shifted around in his chair, trying to find some elusive comfortable position. "Rude, I know, but what the fuck, I'm rude."

"That's an understatement," Daniel said. "One time he dropped me in the woods for two days with no food or water, to see if I could survive. Told me we were going to a strip club."

"You lived, didn't you?" Artie sounded wounded. "And anyway, you'd signed up by then, I wouldn't pull something like that on Marla on such a short acquaintance."

"Stop," Marla said. "Explain what you're talking about. Why am I here?"

"Okay," Artie said. "I was gonna wait until dinner, but I can see how it might be bothering you, and anyway, who wants to watch me talk with my mouth full?" He sat forward in the recliner, leaning closer and looking at Marla, and suddenly the affable fat schlub of a guy seemed much more *there*, his eyes intense and focused, his gaze locked on her. Marla found herself leaning forward herself, listening hard, paying out all her available attention.

"There's a world behind the world," Artie said. "A hidden universe. Dangers you can't imagine, and wonders you won't believe until you see them, and maybe not even then. There are a lot of words for what I am. Wizard. Adept. Magician, but not the kind with mirrors and wires. Magus. Witch. Warlock. The word most of us use around here is sorcerer. From the Latin *sortiarius*, one who influences fortune and fate.

"We work our will to change the world. Some of us use cauldrons and crystal balls and chalk pentagrams on the floor. Some of us use blood and bones and hair. Some of use herbs and potions and sacred rites. Some of us just push as hard as we can against the world and watch the world *move*."

Marla couldn't look away. Artie's voice was simultaneously somehow in her ears and in her head. From the corner of her eye, she could see Daniel, also leaning forward, equally rapt, though he'd surely heard this, or some variation, before.

Artie went on. "But every approach, every specialty, every method is just a personal expression of the fundamental fact: if you have the will, you can change the world. Power like this isn't passed down through families. You don't find a classified ad in the paper. You can't send away for a correspondence course on how to be a wizard—not one that works, anyway. People like me, we keep an eye open for people who have potential. If we see someone who looks promising, someone we like, someone we think we can work with, we sit down with them. Invite them to dinner. Have a little chat." He cleared his throat. "We ask them if they'd like to become an apprentice, and learn to work their will on the world."

Artie sat back again, and the intense moment—magic, or just unsuspected levels of charisma in Artie's personality?—passed. He belched, which further undercut the sense of profundity. "So that's that," he said. "Somebody like you, a teenager, living on the street without getting pulled under by drugs or booze or selling your body, that tells me you're tough as hell. Seeing you handle that guy in the club, seeing you stab Daniel's poppet without a moment's hesitation, that tells me you've got will. Does that mean you'll be able to do magic? I don't know. How'd you like to find out?"

"I don't even know if I believe in magic," Marla said, because it was simple truth. "How do I know you aren't just messing with me, for reasons I can't understand? Trying to trick me, to use me?"

"Let's show her, Artie," Jenny Click said, stepping out of the elevator on the far wall. She wore a red silk dress, simple, short, elegant, and tight, and her hair was the smooth cascading blonde of a classic screen idol's.

She carried a paper bag with a grease stain on the bottom, and there was mud caked on her high heeled shoes and splashed up her bare shins. She stepped across the room and dropped the bag in Artie's lap.

"Any problems with the, ah, delivery?" Artie said.

Jenny shook her head. "Come on, Artie. Let's show her. Like you showed me, when I needed convincing."

"Aw, hell, we were going to eat soon, you must be starving, the afternoon you had—"

"Dinner can wait," Daniel said. "Jenny's right. Marla wants proof. Let's give it to her."

"Okay, okay." Artie gave Marla a long-suffering look. "These kids, they push me around. But why not? So, you want to see some magic?"

"Like last night?" Marla said. "Fireballs and smoke?"

"Nah," Artie said. "I mean, that didn't really convince you, did it? I was thinking of something a little more… incontrovertible."

Daniel rolled his eyes. "Listen to this guy. Incontrovertible. Who's he trying to impress?"

"Okay," Marla said. "Convince me."

Artie nodded. He clapped his hands together, sharply, just once.

And the world changed.

Chapter Four

THERE WAS NO MOMENT of lost consciousness, and not even an eye-blink or a flash of darkness, between Artie's handclap and the transformation of the space around Marla. Such an interval of oblivion might have let her believe she'd been somehow drugged and transported, but the change was instantaneous. One moment, she was sitting on a couch in Artie's living room.

The next, the couch vanished from beneath her and she fell on her ass. She landed on the hard cobblestone street of a foggy city at night, beneath an old-fashioned streetlamp with a curiously flickering light—was that actual *flame* inside the lantern atop the iron pole?

Artie made the transition more gracefully, sitting on the curb beside her, a glass of amber liquid in his hand. "So that was pretty cool, huh? Poof! And shit." Jenny and Daniel were nowhere to be seen. Maybe they hadn't been invited along on this proof-of-concept mission.

Marla stood up with as much dignity as she could muster and looked around. Shuttered shops lined the street, and with the fog she couldn't see much past the end of the block with the fog. Cold, too, and her with no coat. "Where is this? Part of the old city?" Felport had a few cobblestone sections, north of the river in the oldest part of the city, where the streets and shops were all equally ancient and narrow.

"You're not in Felport anymore, Dorothy," Artie said. "This is London, England. Hip, hip, cheerio."

Marla frowned. "Streets in London still have cobblestones, and what…" She kicked the lamppost. "Gaslights?" Wasn't there an old movie, about a guy trying to drive a woman crazy, called *Gaslight*? Was Artie trying to gaslight *her*? Maybe, but that instantaneous transition from here to there, *wherever* here was… that was pretty convincing.

29

"Parts of it, sure, there are gaslights in central London and some of the parks. What, you don't believe we're in England? Why don't you find a local, see if they speak English or not." He grinned. "Actually, this isn't modern London, anyway. It's Victorian-era London."

Marla shook her head. "You almost had me with the teleporting. But you want me to believe you can travel back in time too?"

"Kid, you don't know what you should believe. You've got no context, no way to know what's bullshit and what's plausible. You'll learn, if you decide to stick around. Anyway, I gotta go. I'll see you in a few hours."

She had a lot of practice at playing it cool, but the scramble of panic in her chest was big enough to make her say, "Wait, what? You're leaving me... wherever, whenever, we are? Here? In the past?"

"Sure. You gotta walk around, kick the tires, convince yourself I didn't just drug you and drag you to a soundstage someplace—though why in the hell you think anybody'd expend that much effort to mess with your head is beyond me. I mean, if I really *did* drop you in Victorian England, that would prove something, wouldn't it?"

"Is it safe here?" Marla said.

"Not even remotely. Still got your knife?" He didn't wait for her to answer, just walked off down the sidewalk, taking a theatrically deep breath. "I love the Victorian era. They were so sexually repressed, it twisted them in really interesting ways."

Marla pulled her knife, rushed toward Artie, and gently placed the point in his lower back, about where she thought his kidney was. The knife just dimpled the fabric of his hideous shirt. "You aren't leaving me here. Take me home."

Artie surprised her by simply sprinting forward, moving faster than she believed possible for a man of his size and apparent lack of fitness, and he was well out of strike range before she even thought of actually stabbing him. Artie looked back, *stuck out his tongue at her*, waved, and laughed as he disappeared into the fog. The fat fuck was having fun.

Oh well. What would sticking a knife in him have accomplished, anyway? She'd just be stuck wherever she was with a dead guy at her feet. Might as well do what he suggested. Wander around this place and try to find the seams, the edges, the painted backdrops, the wooden scenery, the smoke machine making this fog. Or, maybe, accept that she was some-where uncanny.

Marla set off, taking turnings at random down quiet streets, peering into windows at cobbler's shops and bakeries and butcher's and candlestick maker's. No one else stirred, and there was no sign of Artie. She'd almost come to believe she really was in the past, in a real city from over a hundred years before, when she encountered something clanking, hissing, and menacing that changed her mind.

"Fuck." She was pretty sure there hadn't been ten-foot-tall robots with iron faces wielding double-headed axes in Victorian England, but now one was advancing toward her from out of the fog, slicing through streetlamps with his axe as it came.

The axe alone was as big as her, and sharp enough to shear through the metal lampposts cleanly. The arms and legs were piston-driven black metal, face a barred metal grate with a single glowing red eye. It was kind of ridiculous looking, really. Also big.

Her knife, on the other hand, suddenly seemed entirely too small. Which meant running away was the proper course of action, though it rankled her.

"Marla, this way!" Jenny Click shouted from somewhere behind her, and Marla spun and ran for the voice. The fact that Jenny was hovering about three feet above the ground, surrounded by a nimbus of flickering orange-yellow flame that lit the fog around her into a fuzzily luminous aura, didn't make Marla pause. Apparently she had a threshold for being taken aback by the impossible, and she'd crossed it in the past few moments. "Duck down that alley," Jenny said, pointing one flame-dripping hand. "I'll take care of this thing."

Marla did as directed, hurrying for a crack of darkness between two leaning brick buildings, though she stopped in the mouth of the alley to see what Jenny would do. She drifted forward like an avenging angel and extended her hands toward the implacable clanking figure. The metal man raised his axe, but the head sagged as the shaft bent, suddenly soft as melting caramel. The metal man dropped the melting weapon and raised hands as big as snow shovels, but its dull black metal body began to glow red, then white, and bolts popped forth from it with a sound like a can of beans exploding in a campfire. A flying bolt pinged off the wall near Marla, knocking loose chips of brick and making her step deeper into the alley, but the projectiles that flew toward Jenny Click wisped away into metal vapor when they reached the aura of her heat.

The metal man's left arm dropped off, and its breastplate clattered steaming to the street, and its red eye cracked and went black. Jenny was still ten feet away from the thing, and it had been reduced to steaming scrap metal.

"Okay," Marla said loudly. "Okay, okay, shit, okay. I believe in magic." She hoped that declaration would be enough, that she would be transported back to Artie's living room, but nothing happened.

Jenny Click descended, feet touching the ground, and the flames haloing her vanished. "Come on," she said, turning toward Marla and, improbably, smiling. "He'll send more soon, let's get out of his territory."

"That thing came from Artie?" Marla stepped out of the alley and walked over to Jenny. The pile of scrap metal popped and pinged as it cooled.

Jenny shook her head. "No, Daniel. It's his specialty—he animates things, gives objects life."

"Why is Daniel trying to kill me with a robot?" Marla wanted to kick the metal remains, but she didn't want to turn her foot into charcoal, so she refrained.

"Just for practice. Come on, let's get into one of the underground stations, that's more my territory." She set off down the street purposefully, still in her mud-spattered heels and evening gown, and Marla had to hurry to keep up.

"Wait, what? There aren't subway stations in Victorian England, Jenny."

"This isn't really London. I'm not supposed to tell you that, probably, but it's not like you wouldn't have figured it out for yourself if you had a moment to think. It's not the past, either. Artie says nobody's ever figured out how to travel back in time, as far as he knows"

"So what is this place, then?"

Jenny shrugged. "Artie made it, with some help from Ernesto. He calls it a pocket universe, a little piece of pinched-off space, furnished with Artie's magic. It's sort of London, but it's a London like you might see in fantasy novels or comic books. Jekyll and Hyde are—is—running around out there somewhere, and Jack the Ripper has a magic talking knife that tells him what to do, and Queen Victoria is a vampire, and there are steam-powered android violinists, and ghost-hunters with monocles, and master criminals who lurk in the sewers with armies of rat men, and monster-worshipping cultists living in the Tower of London, and S&M clubs with women in whalebone corsets wielding whips, and intelligent gorillas who fly zeppelins, and all kinds of crazy stuff. You never know what you're going to get here in Artie's London."

"Okay." Marla was, on the whole, glad she'd only encountered a metal man with an axe, as some of the alternatives sounded worse. "But what's the *point* of this place?"

Jenny laughed. "You're always so pragmatic." She pointed to a set of stairs descending into the sidewalk. "We're going down there. The point is, Artie thinks it's fun, for one thing. For another, this is a place where we can practice our magic without drawing too much attention. Where Daniel can make a giant Frankenstein's monster by stitching together a dozen corpses from the catacombs—yeah, there are catacombs here—without freaking out the ordinaries. Where I can set stuff on fire, *seriously* on fire, without destroying anything real in the process." They descended the stairs into a well-lit space of white tiles and pillars, far more modern-looking than the city above, and Jenny took a seat on one of the benches.

Marla joined her. "So it's like a training ground."

"Yep. Artie's real proud of it. Daniel and I play sort of war games. He sends his poppets, or golems, or whatever you want to call them, against me, and I fight back with fire, mostly. Fire's my specialty. Artie wants us both to learn *more*, too, but he says getting our natural talents under control is a good first step. The stuff I can do… when I started out, when Artie first trained me, I could maybe light a candle, and half the time I'd accidentally melt the candlestick. Now…" She held out her hand, and a flame appeared dancing in the palm of her hand, cycling colors through orange and yellow and red and blue. She closed her fist, and it vanished. "Now I decide what burns."

"But you can only do that stuff here," Marla said slowly, trying to get her head wrapped all the way around it. "It's not really real."

Jenny shook her head. "No. You're wrong. The physical, natural laws here conform to those outside. The magic we learn to work here we can also work in the world. It's just, for some of the bigger effects, we don't *dare*. Artie says there are occasions when you have to use big magic, even at the risk of freaking out the ordinary citizens, because the costs of discretion are too great, but for the most part, keeping a low profile is better. So we do little stuff out there… and learn to do big stuff in here, in case we ever need it. And because knowledge justifies itself."

Something had been bothering Marla, and she tried to think of a way to say it without giving offense, then decided it didn't really matter. "Jenny, don't take this the wrong way, but you seem a lot… smarter now than you used to."

Jenny didn't look mad, or hurt. She just nodded. "I used to have a lot of noise inside my head, Marla. Not so much voices, not usually saying words, but noise—sirens, screeches, klaxons, screaming. Artie says I'm a schizophrenic pyromaniac. But one of the first things he did when he took me on as an apprentice was bring in a healer to quiet down the noise in my head. It's still there, but now I have to listen hard to hear it, and my own thoughts can drown it out." She tapped her temple with her forefinger. "I *think* a lot better now. Learning to control fire helped, too. Knowing I can have a flame whenever I want, that I can look at it without destroying anything, that's a big relief. I don't need to see fire so much, now that I can get it on demand." She took Marla's hand. "I hope you'll join us. I hope you'll let Artie teach you."

"Daniel has his poppets. You've got your flames. What's my special talent supposed to be?"

"Maybe you don't have one," said a voice over the PA system, making Marla flinch.

Jenny rolled her eyes. "Artie, come out! I think she's convinced now."

Artie did his strolling-in-from-nowhere trick, appearing near the subway tracks and walking over. "Hey, kid. You having fun yet?"

Marla was not so easily distracted. "What do you mean, maybe I don't have one?"

Artie sat on the edge of the bench and bumped Marla with his hip, making her move over to give his significantly wider ass some space. "I mean what I said. Daniel and Jenny were both obvious. I mean, Daniel was making rat bones get up and dance around when I found him, using his own life force to animate things, and Jenny was practically crackling— some people can turn their own internal energy into an exothermic reaction and make fire, and if she hadn't come to me, Jenny would've probably been just another weird case of spontaneous human combustion in a few months. But you… you're like me, I think. No twist in your physiology, no natural weirdness, no telepathy or telekinesis or mutant powers or radioactive spiders. Just hard-headedness and determination and will."

He took a cigar out of his shirt pocket and waggled it at Jenny. She snapped her fingers and a flame popped to life on the end. Artie took a deep mouthful of smoke and blew it out happily. "We don't tap into the flow of energies in the world naturally like Jenny and Daniel do. We gotta learn other ways to use energy, to shape the world. There are lots of techniques. You can do rituals to focus the will, you can learn meditation techniques, you can spend long hours slaving over a hot cauldron, you can learn to bargain with the dark and light and morally neutral forces at large in the world… whatever works for you."

Marla was a little disappointed to hear she lacked natural talent. Just her luck—Jenny and Daniel start with supernatural powers out of the box, and she has to scramble to catch up. But then, nothing in her life had ever come easily, and the thought of working hard didn't daunt her in the slightest. "How do you do it?" Marla said. "What's your technique?"

"Sex magic," Artie said.

"Goddamn it, I *knew* this was too good to be true." Marla crossed her arms over her breasts. "I knew you just wanted to use me. Shit, Jenny, you let him fuck you? Does he fuck Daniel too?"

Jenny giggled, and Marla wanted to hit her. She thought this was funny? Maybe she was learning to set shit on fire with her mind, sure, but was that worth being a whore for this fat bastard?

"You got the wrong idea," Artie said. "Look, let me show you something." He stood up, turned to face Marla—his crotch rather disconcertingly right in front of her face—and started to unbutton his pants.

Marla got her knife out. "You better be careful what you show me, Artie. I might just have to cut it off."

"That ship has kinda sailed, kid." Artie dropped his pants. He didn't have on any underwear.

He didn't have a penis, either. Or anything else. His crotch was as smooth and featureless as a doll's.

Chapter Five

"OKAY," MARLA SAID, staring at the smooth blank nothingness of Artie's crotch. "That's... unusual. Were you in an accident or something? Did you aggravate a Doberman?"

"Nah, it was totally intentional." Artie pulled his pants back up and returned to his spot on the bench beside her. "I'm a sex magician, like I said—some people call us pornomancers—but I came up with my own spin on the technique. See, most pornomancers, they get their power from sexual energy in action. They host orgies, use spells to increase libidos, call on sexual loas—like, gods, beings, forces?—for favors, get themselves into the frenzy, even, and pull power from all that." Her shook his head. "But I'm basically a cranky antisocial old fuck, and I didn't like the idea of being dependent on other people having a good time, and the thought of a bunch of people all naked and sticky and thrusting in my house didn't really appeal. So I—"

A slithering thumping noise came from the steps, and Jenny stood up, suddenly wreathed in her aura of fire. A long brownish tubular thing, like a featureless worm made of coarse patchworked fabrics, came down the steps, its head swinging to and fro as if scenting the air. Daniel was seated about halfway down the serpent's twenty-foot length, holding onto a bridle of twisted rope. "I come in peace, Jenny, so flame off," he said. "See, I'm sitting on something totally combustible. We've stopped having war games, I guess?"

Jenny's fire vanished with a faint pop of inrushing air. "We're to the part of the evening where Artie takes his pants down and shows his private parts to Marla."

"Ah, yes. I remember that part. I'm still psychologically traumatized." Daniel climbed off his worm, patting it absently, and the thing slumped motionless, just a rolled heap of fabric now. "You can't possibly understand, you two are girls, but as a guy, seeing that..." He shuddered.

"The sight of a guy with no dick is traumatic for me in a different way," Jenny deadpanned, and Marla actually laughed out loud. Jenny gave her a sly smile and said, "Though it wasn't so bad, since it was Artie. Really it was kind of a relief."

"The shit I put up with from you two," Artie said. "Will you lemme finish explaining here?" He patted Marla's knee, and it was just... companionable. For the first time, she didn't instinctively twitch away from his touch. "Like I was saying, because I like being self-sufficient, but I also like sex a lot, I figured out a way to generate my own magical energy. I'd read all this stuff about the penis thieves of the Congo—"

"Wait, what?" Marla said. "People steal penises? In the *Congo*? What for, to eat? Are they aphrodisiacs?"

Artie waved his hand. "Nah, it's a whole thing, in parts of Africa, people get accused of witchcraft, guys say these evil witches make their penises disappear. It's all bullshit, mass delusion, but some of the so-called witches wind up getting killed by angry mobs, it's messed up. When you make the victims drop their pants and show them that, you know, their penises *haven't* disappeared, they just kind of mutter and say, 'Okay, maybe it's not *gone*, but it's a lot smaller than it used to be, the witches musta shrunk it!'"

Artie shook his head. "Like I said, messed up, but it gave me an idea. I used to fuck any girl who'd have me, and I jerked off about four or five times a day—sorry, probably more than you want to know, but anyway—and I got to thinking about some of the old occult writers, who thought jizz was like a potent emission of life energy, and I thought, why am I wasting that energy on a wad of tissue paper? So... I figured out how to become a magical penis thief of the Congo, right here in Felport. I worked out a spell to make my dick disappear." He spread his hands. "Now I can't jerk off if I want to, I can't fuck, nothing, but I still *want* to, and all that sexual energy just builds up in me... and I can tap that pent-up power to do magic. I bought a bunch of strip clubs and a porno theater, stuff like that, just to rev up the frustration even more. I'm a perpetual living battery of magical power. Funny thing is, sometimes I *do* host orgies, because it drives me crazy seeing people screw on my furniture, and generates even more power."

"You gave up sex for magic?" Marla said.

Artie nodded. "Nobody said the path of a sorcerer was an easy one, Marla. You gotta be willing to make sacrifices. The bigger the sacrifice, sometimes, the bigger the reward. And I can still enjoy good food, booze, basketball games, cracking jokes... And I have enough magical power to create a place like *this*." He waved an arm to encompass the whole imaginary world of his London. "It's a trade-off I'd make again."

"But you made your *dick* disappear," Marla said, ever practical. "How do you pee?"

"It's not really gone. It's invisible, and I can't touch it, or feel it, but it still functions... Look, it's like the opposite of a phantom limb. If you get your arm cut off, you can still *feel* the arm, but it's not really there. Well, I *can't* feel my dick, but it's still there."

"You should see him piss," Daniel said. "It's freaky. This stream of urine just, like, appears from mid-air about three inches from his pelvis."

"Hey," Artie says. "I resent that. It appears at *least* eight inches from my pelvis."

Daniel snorted. "It's been so long since you've seen it you're imagining things. You must be thinking of *my* dick."

"I swear, it's like living in a frat house sometimes." Jenny bumped shoulders against Marla. "I'm glad you'll be living with us now. It'll help balance things out." She paused. "You *are* going to live with us, right? Become an apprentice?"

Marla had been looking for something ever since she ran away from home. She'd hoped for a place where she could exist in peace. She'd barely dared hope for a place where she might belong. "Yeah," she said. "I guess I will."

"Then let's go back home and get some dinner and then..." Artie rubbed his hands together. "Then, the aptitude tests."

Jenny and Daniel both groaned, which made Artie grin wider.

They had dinner around a long rectangular table, with overcooked steaks and undercooked baked potatoes and a lot of laughter, though Marla mostly witnessed the laughter, and didn't much contribute to it, still getting the feel for their group dynamic. Jenny looked a lot less fierce and otherworldly once she changed from her ragged gown into a pink sweatsuit, and Daniel continued to be cute in a way that snagged and nagged at the edges of Marla's attention. While they ate dessert—ice cream, which couldn't be ruined by Daniel's cooking—Marla said, "So does that guy Ernesto live here too?"

Artie glugged from a glass stein of beer, wiped his mouth with his sleeve, and shook his head. "Used to, when he was an apprentice, but he's, uh, graduated, I guess you'd say. He still works for me, but he's got his own place. He's here a lot though."

"How long was he your apprentice?" Marla asked, meaning: How long will I be your apprentice?

"Four, five years? I taught him everything I could. He's learning other stuff on his own, of course. He's another one of those naturally-gifted types, he's got a knack for doing funny things to space/time. You want one of those little magic shops that's bigger on the inside than it looks on the outside, he's your guy."

Marla looked around the table. "So we're, what, the new class of apprentices?"

Artie raised his glass. "Yeah, you could say that."

"Did Ernesto have any... classmates?"

Artie put down his glass. "Okay. I see what you're getting at. Yeah. There were others. Ernesto's the one who didn't wash out." He shrugged. "Some people hit a limit to what they're willing or able to learn. Some people make mistakes so bad, do stuff so dangerous, I have to cut them loose. Some people... Well, magic's dangerous, kid. Some people push too far too fast and don't survive."

"Are the other apprentices dead?"

Both Daniel and Jenny were staring at her, which Marla found annoying. Hadn't it occurred to them to ask these questions? Were they so dazzled to be working magic that they didn't think to ask whether or not they'd survive the course of study?

Artie sighed. "I did good picking you, Marla. A sorcerer's gotta be willing to ask the uncomfortable questions. Yeah. The other ones who came up with Ernesto died. It breaks my heart, but they're gone."

"So is a two-thirds rate of death pretty usual then?"

"Ernesto... he was one of five apprentices."

Marla whistled.

Artie shrugged. "Usually one or two just flake out, go back to ordinary life, or join one of the gangs of half-trained morons running around the city doing thug work for other sorcerers. Ernesto's bunch was especially unlucky. One of 'em was learning to make potions and poisoned herself, she was dead before she dropped the Erlenmeyer flask. Three of the others decided to perform a ritual without checking with me first, and they fucked up the protective circle, and they called up something that, ah... Ate them. Ernesto and me shut the thing up in a little bubble universe about the size of a closet. That was a couple years ago. We both hope it's starved to death by now, but neither one of us wants to check." He spread his hands. "I never said this life was easy. Is it more dangerous than living on the streets? I dunno, maybe not, but the payoff if you survive is a lot—"

"It's okay, I don't need convincing." Marla went back to her ice cream.

"All that, and you aren't *worried* now?" Daniel said, staring at her.

Marla sucked a dollop of vanilla off her spoon. Cold and delicious. "Why worry? So, let's say four out of five apprentices die. I just have to make sure I'm the one who *doesn't*."

"If I get my way, you'll all make it," Artie said. "You're some of the most promising prospects I've seen. And every year that goes by, I become a better teacher." He lifted his glass again. "Here's to beating the odds, huh?"

They toasted, but it was a somewhat restrained affair. Marla didn't get why Daniel and Jenny seemed glum, why Artie looked uncomfortable. She always felt better when she knew what she was up against; it was better than stumbling around in the dark and relying on hope to see you through.

Marla's room was personality-neutral, just a bed, dresser, desk, bookshelf (mostly pop-science books on the universe, the mind, and other such vast subjects) and an armchair, all of far better quality than the stuff in her furnished room at the residential hotel. She had her own bathroom, too, though it was a cramped affair with a shower and a toilet shoved into close proximity, apparently built into the space that used to be a closet. The nicest thing about the room was the bay window with a windowseat looking out, appropriately enough, over the bay. She looked in the dresser and found a variety of clothes in her size, almost all practical—cotton slacks, t-shirts, some men's button-down shirts, good workaday clothes. There was even a sock-and-underwear drawer with nothing too outlandish.

In the bottom drawer, she found a bunch of lacy complex underthings in red and black and white and blue, with some items that would have made the strippers at the Bau Bau Room widen their eyes and shake their heads. They were probably her size; she didn't check. She opened her bedroom door and hurled the whole drawerful into the hallway. That should get the point across.

Marla stretched out on the bed, contemplated the ceiling, and waggled her fingers at the overhead light. "Poof," she said. "Abracadabra," she said. "Let there be dark," she said.

When none of that achieved anything, she got up, flipped off the light switch, and went to sleep.

She was awakened the next morning by a thumping knock at the door. Weak gray light showed in the window, though the sun wasn't over the horizon yet. Artie yelled through the door, "Breakfast in fifteen minutes, then get ready for the hardest day of your life!"

"Okay," she called, swinging her legs out of the bed. She'd always had a knack for waking up quickly, though a shower and food would help the process.

"What's with the pile of hooker underwear in the hallway?" Artie's voice was muffled through the door.

"Uh, yeah—not to be ungrateful, but it's not my style, I mean, thanks anyway—"

"Shit, *I* didn't leave that stuff in your room, kid. Drop it down in the costume closet before you come to eat, I'm not your maid."

Huh. If Artie hadn't left her that stuff, who had? Jenny wouldn't have done it, so… Daniel?

Interesting. Maybe offensive, but interesting.

It wasn't the hardest day of her life—the day, at age fourteen, that her brother helped her bury a body, that was the hardest, and probably always would be—but it was a close second.

The sun had been down for two hours by the time Artie said, "Okay, that's enough for today," and let Marla go into the living room to collapse on the couch. She was soaked with sweat, had a raging headache, her fingers ached, her throat was dry, her ears were ringing, and she hadn't achieved a single good goddamn thing.

They'd started out testing her psychic prowess, using Zener cards and various guessing games, Artie very patiently explaining meditative techniques, mind-opening tricks, and offering constant encouragement. Marla had turned out to be roughly as psychic as an axe handle.

The next aptitude tests were a lot more exhausting, and were variations on the same idea that prompted them to let Daniel's poppet attack her in the hallway—under extreme stress, sometimes the magically-gifted spontaneously showed their powers. So they went to Artie's London, where she was pursued for the greater part of the day by nightmarish monsters through dank sewer tunnels, cramped tower rooms, and cells haunted by the souls of executed traitors. She did battle with the mindless vampire-slave guards of Buckinham Palace and crept through alleyways pursued by the Ripper and his whispering knife. When it came to stabbing, improvising weapons, being sneaky, and kicking downed enemies in the head, Marla showed great ability and ingenuity—but she didn't enact a single bit of magic.

Back in the real world she failed to notice the presence of a ghost Artie kept in a jar; failed to see any meaningful pattern in the swirl of ink in a bowl or the configuration of tea leaves in a cup or the guts of a dead rooster on a butcher block; failed to make any accurate guesses about the original owner of an antique silver compass; failed to shield her mind from a psychic intrusion; failed to move a pencil or ignite a candle or snuff a candle by thought alone; and failed to understand the recorded language of any number of animals, among other disappointments.

The only thing she *did* succeed at was maintaining a motionless meditative pose while a monstrous cacophony of clanging blaring brain-shaking noise exploded all around her. She'd grown up with a promiscuous drunk mother in a house with thin walls; she'd had a lots of practice at ignoring loud distractions.

Artie sat down beside her on the couch and handed her a glass of ice tea. "How you doin'?"

She shook her head. "Not good, I guess. So I'm not telekinetic, psychic, necromantic, pyrokinetic, precognitive, clairvoyant, psychometric, empathetic, psycholinguistic, I can't see auras, talk to animals, communicate with spirits, or even pull a rabbit out of a hat. So… I fail. At everything."

"Nah. You're really good at concentrating and beating the shit out of stuff."

She shook her head. "Fat lot of good that does me."

"You didn't wash out today, Marla. The point of these tests was to see if you had any natural, inborn ability—like Daniel's manipulation of life force, or Jenny's explodiness. But, you know… it looks like you don't. You got a lot of gifts, I think, just not magical ones."

"So I'm not special, like they are. Where does that leave me?"

"Don't worry about it. Some people are born with perfect pitch, sure—but just because you don't have perfect pitch doesn't mean you can't learn to *sing*."

"But I'm equally bad at everything!"

"Okay, but on the other hand, you're equally *good* at everything. Look, sorcerers like to specialize, because we can be an obsessive bunch, and also because there's some truth to the notion that if you dig deeper and deeper into a particular discipline, you can discover new and amazing things. Maybe you'll find something that really fits for you eventually, but in the meantime, let's act like you're in college and you don't know what the hell you want to do with your life, can't figure out a major—so you just take a lot of classes until something lights your fire. We'll teach you a little bit of everything."

Marla nodded glumly. "And what if I never find something I'm really good at?"

"There's nothing wrong with being a utility infielder, a jill-of-all-trades. There's a writer I like, guy named Heinlein, who says a human being should be able to do all kinds of things, from changing a diaper to running a war to building a house to sailing a ship. 'Specialization is for insects,' he says. If you learn a little bit of everything, Marla, you'll practically be a specialist *anyway*—most sorcerers are pretty much crap outside their chosen field. Adaptability isn't a bad thing."

"But—"

He put his hand on her shoulder. "Kid. You're *just like me*. I couldn't do anything out of the box, either. But I'm stubborn as hell and I don't know the meaning of quit. And look at me now. Some of the shit I can do, you *still* wouldn't believe if I told you. Sure, Jenny and Daniel have their natural talents, they've got perfect pitch, they can sing real sweet—but you, you'll be able to sing a little, dance a little, do some juggling, ride a unicycle. You'll be like an octuple-threat. Okay?"

Marla'd had such a rough day, she felt herself relax a little for the first time in she couldn't remember how long, and she rested her head on Artie's shoulder. "Okay." She paused. "It's just… failing at anything really pisses me off."

"Good. Anger is a wonderful engine." Artie ruffled her hair. "Tomorrow, I'll teach you to make a magical light, so you can always push back the darkness."

Chapter Six

WHEN MARLA DRAGGED HERSELF upstairs to her room and opened the door, she groaned. Daniel was lounging on her bed, flipping through a big hardcover book, looking relaxed and cool and not at all battered, sweaty, or defeated. "Off. Out. Get. Go. Sleep now."

Daniel closed the book and looked at her from beneath his long eyelashes—boys always did get the best eyelashes, Marla's brother was the same way. "How'd your aptitude tests go?"

Marla walked to the bed, grabbed hold of his ankles, and jerked him off the bed onto the floor. He never lost his grin, even when his head thumped on the carpet. Marla climbed into bed and pulled the covers over her head.

"That well, huh?" he said. "I know you're tired, but are you sure you don't want to change into some… other sleepwear?"

Marla rolled over and gave him a glare containing all her strength—which, alas, was not very considerable at the moment. "You left that lacy crap for me? In your dreams, Daniel. I'm not that kind of girl."

"Can't blame a guy for hoping. Or dreaming. Sleep well, Marla."

"Be lucky if I sleep at all, sore as I am," she said, though her eyes were already drooping.

He reached out and touched her head. "Poor you. Wouldn't want you to miss out on your beauty sleep."

At first, she thought his hand was wet, that he was pulling some sophomoric prank and dumping water on her head, but then the coolness of his touch spread down her spine and through her limbs, and where the cool touched, her aches ceased. She wasn't numbed—the pain was just *gone*.

Marla sat up fast and batted his hand away. "What did you do?"

Now his grin faltered. "Just gave you a little jolt of life, and undid all the damage you did to your body today. No need to thank me—"

"Idiot," she said. "Don't ever do that again. Don't you know anything about exercise? I'm *supposed* to be sore. I pushed myself hard today, and my muscles are full of little microtears from the effort. Those little tears get filled in with new muscle as they heal—and that's how you get *strong*. And you... you just poofed it away with magic and undid my whole day's work! I won't be any stronger tomorrow than I was this morning!" And given that she hadn't accomplished anything *but* physical exertion today, the loss of that tiny bit of conditioning was even more disheartening.

"You know, Marla," Daniel said evenly, "You can be kind of a bitch."

"Sure." She felt less sleepy now—probably another side-effect of him giving her "life." Whatever that meant. Where did he take the life *from*? "A girl who doesn't giggle and flip her hair when you walk by is a bitch, right? You can get by on charm and long eyelashes and a cute butt, but we don't all have those gifts. Some of us have to fight and kick and claw to get along in the world, Daniel."

He shook his head. "You don't know what I've had to do to get here, Marla. Don't think you do." He started to leave, but paused in the doorway. "Your butt's not so bad, by the way." He turned off her light and shut the door after him.

It was, she thought a little sadly in the dark, probably the nicest thing a cute boy had ever said to her.

The next morning came too soon, but at least Artie didn't roust her out of bed before dawn. She went down to the dining room, where a few bagels and a plate of burnt-to-charcoal bacon awaited her. Artie was eating a breakfast burrito as big around as a mortar shell and reading a racing form, Jenny was picking at half a grapefruit, and Daniel, as far as she could tell, was living on air and coffee. They mumbled good mornings.

"So what's on the agenda for today?" She poured a cup of coffee and took a sip. She'd had worse, but only once, at a truck stop outside Chattanooga. Give this pot another hour of sitting on the burner and it would win the prize. "You all take turns hitting me with oars from a canoe?"

"Nope. You got a driver's license, Marla?" Artie didn't look up from his form.

"Sure. Rollo made it for me."

Artie snorted. "You know how to drive though?"

"Yeah."

"Good. You and Daniel go out to the airport." He passed a piece of paper over to her. "Flight number's there. You're picking up a friend of mine, guy named Lao Tsung. Bring him back here."

"Sure thing." Gofer work. Ah, well. Chop wood, carry water. "Where's the car?"

"Daniel will show you. Just don't let him behind the wheel."

"I could drive," Daniel said.

"Not after last time." Artie glanced at his watch, an ostentatious thing of chunky gold. "Okay, Jenny my dear. You ready?"

She nodded and stood up, and Marla whistled. Jenny had on a white blouse, which would have been conservative if it hadn't hugged her boobs so tight, and a plaid ruffled skirt and knee socks. "Are you starring in some schoolgirl porn or something?"

Jenny rolled her eyes and nodded. "I know, right? There's a Catholic school, and they actually dress like this, for *serious*. I'm, ah—" She glanced at Artie.

He shrugged. "Marla's in the family now, you can tell her. But the short form, we gotta get going, and so do they."

"I'm going undercover at St. Luke's. I'm a senior, apparently." She dropped a cursty. "The new librarian there is a sorcerer from out west, traveling incognito, and Artie wants to know why he's taking a job at a private Catholic school. Maybe there's some old text hidden away in the library or something, who knows?"

"Maybe he's just got a schoolgirl fetish," Marla said.

"Nah, that's more my speed." Artie wiped his mouth and tossed his napkin onto the table. "We're gone. You two." He pointed at Daniel and Marla in turn. "Be polite to Lao Tsung. Respectful, even. He doesn't have a sense of humor like I do. I'll see you all back here in a few hours."

They left, and as soon as the elevator trundled up to the ground level, Daniel said, "Give me the keys."

"Blow me," Marla said.

"I think that's my line."

The car was the Bentley again, tucked away in a garage not far from the front door, but so cunningly built against the hill and into the landscape that it was barely noticeable if you weren't looking for it—Marla wondered if there was some magic on the place to deter the eye.

Marla started it up, sighed, and reversed out of the garage. She didn't like driving, and hadn't done it much. Things went by too quickly behind the wheel of a car. It was hard to pay attention to anything but the bare necessities of staying on the road, not crashing, and obeying traffic laws; the peripheral became a blur, and she worried, always, about missing something that mattered.

Daniel directed her toward the coast road and north, the bay a vastness on one side, forests soon appearing on the other, the city left behind. "I understand why I'm being sent to fetch someone," Marla said. "I don't know how to *do* anything yet. But why aren't you out committing crimes like Jenny?"

"Oh, the same reason Artie won't let me drive. I'm being punished." He stared out the passenger window at the water, and she envied him the sustained view, which she could only see in quick glances.

"Punished for what?"

Daniel shrugged. "I sorta drove off a cliff."

"Sorta?"

"Okay. Totally. Totally off the cliff. Just up here, actually, see where there's a new shiny length of guardrail? That's because I broke through the old faded guardrail."

The spot he pointed out wasn't in a curve, or at the bottom of a hill, or anything, just an unremarkable place in a straight length of two-lane blacktop. "Was it an accident?" Marla asked.

"No, I did it on purpose. Artie was with me, I knew he wouldn't let us drown. I wanted to see how he'd handle it. He's always testing us, so I figured, it was only fair, I'd test *him*. Just jerked the wheel hard and off we sailed." He smiled a little. "There's a moment when you feel weightless, when momentum keeps you in the air. Then gravity takes hold."

Childish, Marla thought, though she could see the appeal of messing with Artie. After what he'd put her through yesterday, especially. "Since you're not dead and the car's still here, I guess he saved you. What did he do?"

"I don't know, exactly. We busted through the guard rail and fell toward the bay, all that gray water rushing up at us, and Artie just, like, sighed. He said I shouldn't waste his time, then thumped me on the side of the head—not hard, must've been some magic in his fingers—and I woke up soaking wet on the sand about three hours later with some kind of crab nibbling my toes. But when I hiked back to the house, the car was there, not a drop of water on it, so Artie did *something*."

"Should've made it look like an accident," Marla said. "I would've acted like the brakes weren't working, and I would have crashed through up here, where the road curves, see? Like it was unavoidable. Then Artie might not have knocked you out."

"Not bad. But it's easy to point out the flaws in someone else's plan."

"It doesn't sound like you actually had a plan. You just… did some shit."

She glanced over at him, and his eyes were narrowed, and he looked pissed off, and she thought, *Okay, he's that kind of guy,* but then he laughed. "Yeah, yeah, touché. About ninety percent of what I do I just do on impulse. Not you, huh? Gotta figure all the angles first, right?"

"I have impulses." She considered jerking the wheel and going off the cliff just to prove Daniel wrong… except she didn't have that much faith in his magical abilities. He could probably make the car glow green and drive itself without the engine running, but she had doubts about his ability to make it fly.

"Do you ever have… impulses… about me? Dirty ones?" He waggled his eyebrows, and Marla had known enough boys to guess he'd pretend to be joking if she laughed at him, but if she showed any interest…

"Do you harass Jenny this way and I just don't see it? Or are you afraid she'll set you on fire?"

"Jenny?" He made a thppt sound. "She's like my sister or something. Not my type, anyway."

"Blonde, pretty, capable of levitation? That's not your type? And I'm supposed to believe *I* am?"

"Look, I like Jenny—I love her, she's basically family after the months we've spent together—but she's got pretty much zero sense of humor, and even though she's a lot more… mentally together than she used to be… most of her conversations still revolve around fire, or Artie, or setting stuff on fire for Artie. I can tell you're smart, you ask good questions, I don't know, I'm just interested in getting to know you better."

"Really? Because I got the impression you were mostly interested in sleeping with me. The lingerie, the innuendo, doesn't seem like you wanted a meeting of the minds, Daniel." The road curved away from the bay, turning inland, and the forest gave way to fields.

"Okay, I was a little crass. What can I say. I don't do subtle. I like watching you beat stuff up. I like how you move. Makes me wonder how you'd move if you weren't beating stuff up."

"I'm flattered. I am. But dial it back a little, would you? You piss me off some, but you don't bore me, so call that part a draw. And you're not bad to look at. I don't know how I feel about touching, though. My life is pretty complicated right now. I'm... adjusting."

"Fair enough. We've got a long time to get to know each other better. But if you ever want to give in to your impulses and just make out for a while, you know where to find me."

It was, Marla decided, an option to keep in mind.

They parked the Bentley in the short term lot and loitered near the departures area, Daniel holding up a sign that read "Lao Tsong." Eventually a man came toward them, lean and sinewy with black hair in a ponytail and vaguely Asian features. He was no taller than Marla, probably about 40 years old, and wearing travel-rumpled black casual clothes. A nasty-looking hand-rolled cigarette hung unlit in the corner of his mouth, and he stopped in front of them for a long moment, then tapped his forefinger on the sign. "Spelled wrong. It's 'Tsung,' with a 'u.'"

"Ah, sorry," Daniel said. "Artie didn't spell it for us."

Lao shrugged. "It's okay. I'll kick your ass for it later, we'll call it even. Where's the car? You better get me to Artie's before I need to take a shit. I hate public toilets." He walked toward the outer doors without waiting for them to lead, or even follow.

Marla looked at Daniel, who shrugged, and they went after him. "How was your flight?" she asked, and then added, "sir," because of what Artie said about respect.

"Sir?" Lao said without looking back, striding through the crosswalk against the light. As Marla hurried after him, narrowly avoiding death by taxi, she realized Lao didn't have any bags. She also realized he was walking unerringly toward the spot where they'd parked the car. He'd probably been here before, knew where the short-term parking was, but still, it was a big lot...

"Sir! Don't sir me. What's Artie been telling you? He knows I turned down that knighthood. Death to the monarchy!" He reached the Bentley, patted the roof with his open hand as if greeting a beloved pet, and turned. "My flight was shit. The only thing worse than flying across the ocean in an airplane is flying by magic." He shook his head. "You kids better be worth all the trouble Artie's putting me through."

"I'm... what?" Daniel said.

"I'm here for *you*," Lao said. "To toughen you up! Teach you a thing or two! Put hair on your chests!" He eyed Marla. "Not yours. Probably. We'll take it on a case by case basis." He played a rapid drumbeat tattoo on the roof of the car. "Give me the keys, and let's roll till the rolling's done."

"Oh, we can drive," Daniel said, "You must be jetlagged, you don't want to drive when you're tired, your reflexes—"

Marla barely saw Lao move, but Daniel was flat on his back, and Lao was kneeling beside him, one hand cupped on the back of Daniel's head, holding it half an inch above the pavement. "Reflexes. You see those reflexes? Knocked you down *and* kept you from cracking your skull. Those are my *jetlagged* reflexes. You just wait."

"Artie said to show you respect," Marla said. She tossed the car keys, which Lao snatched out of the air without rising, or even looking up. "Respect."

"You, I like." Lao stood and prodded Daniel's ribs with his toe. "You, I don't like so much. But you can get up."

Daniel rose, gingerly, as if unsure whether or not all his limbs were still attached.

"Huh," Marla said, going around to the passenger side; no question in her mind she would be riding shotgun. "Usually nobody likes me. Usually everybody likes Daniel."

"I'm a contrary motherfucker," Lao said, and climbed into the car.

"Lao is an expert in… well, fifteen, twenty thousand different things." It was evening, and Artie was in an expansive playing-host mood, sitting on his overstuffed white couch with a cigar in his hand. Lao sat cross-legged on the teak coffee table in the center of the conversation area, smoking a disgusting handrolled cigarette, which, by the smell, was more ditchweed than tobacco. Jenny—who had a bruise on her forehead Marla was curious about—was in an armchair, fluorescing a little in her school-girl outfit, her fiery aura resonating to the tiny little sources of flame. *All we need is for Daniel to start puffing on a corncob pipe and set off the smoke alarms and this will be loads of fun,* Marla thought.

She was beside Daniel on the couch with Artie. Lao Tsung was facing them but not, apparently, paying them any attention, dividing his time between contemplating the ceiling and examining his cigarette for signs of paper fatigue.

"But right now," Artie went on, "Lao Tsung is here in his capacity as an ass-kicking expert. Master of every martial art from aikido to, fuck if I know, zen-fu, whatever. He's gonna teach you three how to throw a punch and take a punch and, if you're good, maybe some fancy shit like how to punch a guy so his testicles explode ten minutes later."

"He's a self-defense teacher?" Daniel said. "But we can do *magic*—at least, Jenny and me can, no offense, Marla. Jenny can make a guy's testicles explode *without* punching him, and I can... well. You know what I can do. Why should we waste our time learning to kick people when we could be learning the inner secret sacred mysteries?"

"Why?" Artie leaned over and tapped a chunk of cigar ash onto Daniel's knee. "Because sometimes magic doesn't help. Because you're tired. Or because you're up against a sorcerer who's as good as you are—or better. At this point, kid, most of them are better than you, believe me. You try and do some spell and they just brush it off like a cobweb and start working up a little magic of their own, and you're screwed. But if you know how to hit them in the throat so they choke on their own windpipe, they can't exactly finish the incantation, can they? I want you three to learn to fight because most apprentices *don't*, and being able to sweep the leg and kick the ass will give you an edge a lot more often than you think."

He sat back and regarded Daniel, benignly to all appearances, though Marla wondered. "Now, I explained that to you because I believe in an open and honest dialogue about our thoughts, feelings, hopes, and ideals, but really, the only reason you should need is, 'Because Artie says so.' If it weren't for me... You know where you'd be, Daniel. Your hillbilly relatives would've put a stake through your heart and stuffed your mouth with garlic and cut off your head and buried you at a crossroads, and the only reason they wouldn't have shot you with silver bullets is because they couldn't afford the silver. Am I right?"

Marla had never seen Daniel furious before. Peeved, sure, sarcastic, certainly, but now his eyes were like dying embers and his mouth was set in a hard line that was less frown and more a barely contained snarl. Marla tensed up in unintentional sympathy.

Then Daniel sighed. "You're right, Artie. Sorry." And some of the tension bled out of the room.

Marla said, "So you're a secret martial arts master too, then, Artie?"

"Fuck no. I can hit a guy with a pool cue when he ain't looking, but beyond that, I don't fight. That's why I've got apprentices who know how to fight, see?"

Daniel laughed. "So when do we start this ass-kicking training?"

"Now," Lao said, and launched himself off the table.

Chapter Seven

LAO TSUNG'S BODY HIT DANIEL hard enough to tip the couch over on its back, and Marla went sprawling too—though Artie, somehow, got gracefully out of the way. Probably the same trick he used to stroll in out of nowhere. Marla used her momentum to turn her fall into an inelegant back roll, and regained her feet near the fireplace.

Lao squatted over Daniel's chest, pinning him down. "Preparedness," he said. "You have to always—"

Marla stepped forward and smacked Lao on the side of his head as hard as she could, boxing his ear. Her hand stung from the impact, but he barely seemed to notice.

Lao turned his head to her and grinned—his somber face was transformed by the goofy smile. "She gets the idea," Lao said. "But next time, Marla, don't hold your hand flat, it's more effective if you do this—"

In an instant he was off Daniel and standing in front of her, arms swinging around to slam his loosely-cupped hands against both her ears simultaneously. Marla staggered back, her sense of balance utterly undone. She turned, tried to catch herself, and tripped over the edge of the fireplace, falling onto her hands and knees. Marla looked up at Lao, who continued lecturing. "That's an ear slap. Requires hardly any training, hurts and disorients, very useful for beginners. Much better than punching someone in the head, because hitting a skull with your fist is a good way to break your hand. Now—"

Jenny jumped onto Lao from behind, wrapping her arms around his neck, and Lao paused for a moment, then shook his head. "There are blood chokes, where you squeeze the artery and cut off the blood supply to the brain and knock someone unconscious. Fairly safe if done right. There are air chokes—much more dangerous—where you cut off the air supply, but sometimes you might accidentally crush the windpipe if you don't know what you're doing. But you, Jenny, are just getting in your own way, you aren't using your leverage at all. It's okay. I'll show you the right way later."

He reached back and grabbed Jenny by the—head? shoulders? Marla couldn't tell from her angle, down here on the floor. Lao bent at the waist, as if doing a little bow, and flipped Jenny over his shoulder like she weighed no more than a pillow, slamming her supine on the carpet.

"Ow," Jenny said, staring up at the ceiling. Marla struggled upright. One hit—okay, technically two—and her head was still spinning and her breakfast was threatening to come back out through the in door. Artie was leaning back against a wall, just watching—impossible to tell if he was pleased or disappointed or what.

"Screw punching," Daniel said, appearing behind Lao Tsung and laying a hand on his shoulder. A greenish glow surrounded Daniel, and Lao Tsung sagged slightly as the light spread to envelop him. Then Lao grinned again, and the green turned first yellowish and then white, and Daniel gasped and stepped back, shaking his head in confusion, or dibelief, or both. Though he'd broken physical contact with Lao, the light still connected them, stretching like sticky strands of egg yolk between their bodies, like threads of saliva connecting two sets of lips after a messy kiss. It was one of the weirdest things Marla had ever seen—and she'd seen Artie with his pants down.

Lao turned, the light shifting around him. He looked at Daniel for a moment, then kicked him almost casually in the inner thigh, halfway up from the knee. Daniel screamed and fell to the ground, clutching at his leg, and the white light vanished. "There's a nerve cluster in the thigh, really sensitive. Even a pinch there hurts pretty had. A kick like that... don't try to stand up too soon." Lao squatted beside Daniel and pushed down on his shoulder, making him lay flat on his back. He spoke softly. "Trying to pull the life out of me back there was rude. You didn't see Jenny trying to set me on fire—she understood what we were doing, what the point was. You were not only rude, but kind of stupid. Or did you think you're the only person who knows how to manipulate *qi*?"

"We've been calling it *prana*," Artie said. "I dunno if Daniel knows *qi* from a hole in his head."

Lao Tsung shrugged. "They're basically the same concept. Life force. Energy flow. The universal breath. Learn to manipulate that, and you can take life, give life, heal sickness, cause disease." He slapped Daniel's cheeks lightly, as if to keep his attention. "I wasn't born with that power, like you. I spent decades studying to learn to manipulate *qi*. But because I've studied, I'm better than you are." He sat on his heels. "I am not, probably, better than you'll ever be—not if you practice. If you behave, and try to learn the practical, physical things I'm teaching you about self defense, I'll show you some of what I know about *qi*. Can we agree?"

Marla waited to see what Daniel would say. He was proud, she knew that, but surely he'd have the sense to see this more as an opportunity than an embarrassment? If he didn't, she'd lose all respect—

"Agreed," Daniel said, sitting up. "Sorry about all that. It's just… habit. Instinct, even. I've been trained to use my power to fight. Artie taught me that."

"Sure." Lao nodded. "But when you tried, and it failed, you didn't have anything to fall back on." He stood and offered Daniel his hand, pulling the boy to his feet. "I'm here to fix that. We'll—"

Marla hit Lao in the back of the head with a poker from the fireplace. Daniel, who'd seen her coming, hadn't let a flicker of expression appear on his face while she approached, but once she struck, he smiled.

"I really like this girl, Artie," Lao said, and fell forward onto his face.

Over the next weeks, Marla settled into a routine. She would wake roughly at dawn, eat breakfast, and then train with Lao Tsung until lunch. Daniel was there about three-quarters of the time, Jenny maybe half— they did other jobs for Artie, the details of which Marla only heard about vaguely. She vibrated with jealousy, but tried to make sure no one noticed. Her time, she hoped, would come.

Lao's lessons had become a bit more formal—no more jumping on them unawares in the living room; they used Artie's surprisingly-well equipped subterranean gym—but they were no less grueling. Because Marla was there more often, and because she had a knack for physicality, she learned more about fighting than the other apprentices.

She was glad to have any edge she could get, because after lunch, she studied with Artie, or took lessons from Ernesto, or—humiliatingly—Daniel and Jenny. Magic was not coming to her easily. She was, she learned, not even really an apprentice yet—she was a trainee, on probation, or a frosh, depending on which of her teachers was teasing her. If she proved completely hopeless at magic, she understood, it wouldn't matter how well she kicked people or swung a sword—Artie would have to cut her loose. Until she mastered the basic magical competencies, her place was a lot more uncertain than she liked.

After valiant effort she learned to light a candle with a word—Artie said the incantation was an insult to the air, particles gyrating in anger fast enough to spark flame, and she wasn't sure if he was kidding. She learned other tricks, which Ernesto dismissively classed as cantrips—opening doors from across a room, rotting wood, rusting metal, things like that.

"This is bullshit," she said after four months, when she'd failed, for the tenth time that morning, to make a flower wilt by staring at it. "I've got no feel for the *qi* or *prana* or whatever, it's just words to me." She shoved back from the dining room table in frustration.

"Keep trying." Artie patted her shoulder. "You'll get it."

"So what if I do? I can kill a flower. Big whoop."

"I know these seem like small steps, but the thing to remember is, you're getting into the habit of imposing your will on the world. That's important. Do you think you could move a mountain with your will alone?"

She snorted. "I can barely shove a coffee mug across the table."

"Yeah, but when you started, you couldn't shift a thumbtack, or roll a pencil, and you've got that down now, right?"

"Only because you made me practice it a million times!"

"Don't make me get pedagogical on your ass, Marla." Artie pulled out a chair and sat beside here. "I'm a believer in what's called 'overlearning.' You practice something again and again and again, dozens and scores and hundreds and thousands of times, until it's totally ingrained, until you can do it without even thinking about it. That's how your magic should be. Casting a spell should be like shifting a muscle, no distance between thought and action."

"Just like fighting, huh?"

"Same idea. Drill, and drill, and drill, until you just *know* it, no question. The point is, every little step builds your confidence. First you move a thumbtack with your mind, and then it doesn't seem impossible to move a pencil, so you move that. Then a comb seems possible, then a toy car, then a coffee mug, and eventually a shoe, a bowling ball, a toaster oven, a chair, a refrigerator, a car, a house, an office building… a mountain." He shrugged. "You'll get there. You've got the will, and the tenacity."

She nodded. "I get it. But even that's just telekinesis. There are so many other things I want to learn, so many other disciplines, how do I even know what I should be focusing on?"

"It's a question," Artie allowed. "What kind of martial art is Lao teaching you?"

Marla laughed. "You might as well call it Lao fu. I asked once, and he said, 'Oh, kung-fu, with some judo, and aikido. And a little savate. And jeet kune do, but that's mostly just wing chun and fencing and boxing anyway. Oh, and obnu bilate for the stick fighting, and defendu, which is really just modified jujutsu...' He went on like that for about twenty minutes. I was sorry I asked."

"The foul rag and bone shop method," Artie said.

Marla frowned. "What?"

"It's from a Yeats poem. 'The foul rag and bone shop of the heart.' Yeats was talking about all the stuff writers draw on to create their art, the messy disordered junk in their psyches that they sort through and turn into poetry, but the same idea can apply to magic, or martial arts, or whatever. You take a bunch of disparate elements and turn them into something elegant and beautiful. That's the kind of sorcerer you're going to be, Marla—a foul rag and bone shop sorcerer, using whatever comes to hand, but making it beautiful." He brushed her bangs out of her face—she'd been meaning to get it cut short, but hadn't gotten around to it yet. "I can't wait to see what you become, kid. I've been thinking, though, and I know what you should learn next. Where you should really focus your attention."

"What's that?"

"Well, you're stubborn as hell, and you don't mind putting in long hours, and you like punching people, so let's combine the two. I'm going to teach you 'chanting. It takes a lot of time, and a lot of precision, and doing a whole lot of steps exactly right, but when it works, you can make some pretty awesome stuff."

"Awesome would be a nice change," Marla said.

Marla had been with Artie for nearly nine months—it was summer in Felport, not that she'd been out in the weather much—when she dropped the pair of brass knuckles on Artie's desk in his study. "There," she said. "I got it, finally."

Artie took off his reading glasses and put aside a sheaf of papers. She wondered if the glasses were an affectation; couldn't he just magically fix his own vision? Her mind was wandering. She'd been up all night, and not for the first time. She tried to focus. Today could be the day.

Artie picked up the brass knuckles and slid them onto the fingers of his right hand. "Let's see." He rose and left the room, and Marla followed him down to the gym, where Lao Tsung was holding what amounted to a remedial martial arts class for Jenny and Daniel, who'd been out in the field more and more lately, doing who knows what kind of exciting and violent things.

"Gather 'round," Artie said. "Marla's got her apprentice piece done." He held up his fist, brass knuckles gleaming. "Lao, set up the test?"

"Sure thing." Lao piled up several concrete paving stones until he had a stack a few feet high. Marla had practiced breaking on those stones, though not often, because Lao considered brick breaking silly stuff mostly good for showing off at demonstrations. She'd never tried to hit a stack that thick, piled all together directly on the floor with no space beneath, either. She didn't think it would be possible... unless she'd done her job right.

"Okay," Artie said, as the others gathered around to watch "Here goes." He lifted his arm high, elbow cocked, back, then drove his fist down onto the concrete, dropping to one knee as he went.

The blocks more or less exploded on impact, Jenny puffing out a temporary shield of heat to vaporize the shrapnel. When the dust settled, Artie was unmoving, his fist pressed flat against the floor, the paving stones two tottering piles on either side of his hand.

"Power's there," Artie said. He held up his hand, considering it carefully, turning it in the light. After entirely too long a moment—during which Marla held her breath—he said, "The impact didn't hurt, and there's not a scratch on my hand. Good combination of power and defense." He pulled off the brass knuckles and tossed them to Marla, who caught them, allowing herself to breathe again. "You've just done your first successful piece of enchanting."

Suddenly Jenny was hugging her, and Daniel and Lao were slapping her on her back, and Artie was grinning. "Welcome to the family, kid," he said. "You're a real apprentice now." He cleared his throat. "Or you will be, once we do the loyalty oath."

Marla looked up from her enchanted weapon, frowning. "What?"

"It's okay, Marla," Jenny said. "Daniel and I both did it. And Ernesto before us."

"Think of it as a combination non-compete clause and insurance policy." Artie spoke while squatting to chalk a red symbol on the floor. "Basically, it's a promise—but a magical, unbreakable promise—that we'll look out for each other. Think of it like... we're NATO. An act of aggression against one of us is an act against all."

"Don't bullshit her, Artie," Lao said. "It's a geas. She should know it's serious."

"Geese?" Marla looked from Artie to Lao.

"Geas." Artie spelled it, still drawing. "A... magical compulsion. If, say, somebody kills me, you'll have a powerful urge to avenge me. Same thing happens to me if somebody kills *you*. It's insurance. Other sorcerers know if they mess with you, I'm on their ass, and vice-versa."

"Tell her what happens if she doesn't avenge you," Lao said.

"You go crazy and die, okay?" Artie said. "But that's only if you don't even *try*. And the same thing happens to me if you go down and I don't do anything about it. Okay? And if for some reason we decide to part ways, that we don't wanna go to the mattresses for each other anymore, we can mutually agree to remove the geas, do another ritual like this one, and take it away. If you want an escape hatch, that is."

"You all did this?" Marla said. "Jenny, Daniel, Lao?"

"Not me." Lao shook his head. "I'm an old friend and a well-paid employee, but this..."

"This is like... family." Marla nodded to herself. "Like family is supposed to be. Taking care of each other, no matter what. Making promises and keeping them." Her own family was nothing like that. Absent unknown father, drunken mother, and even her closest relation, her brother, was... complicated. "Sure. I'll do it. You three are my family now."

"That's what I want to hear," Artie said. "Let's step into this circle and say the words, kid."

"Here you go." After dinner, Artie pushed a wrapped box across the table to her. "Graduation gift."

"Only took you nine months," Daniel said, grinning over his ice cream. "That's as long as it takes to grow a *baby*."

"Open it, Marla!" Jenny said, clapping her hands.

Marla tore the bright paper off the box, opened it up, and beheld...

A pair of black, beautiful, supple leather boots. Not girly boots like the ones in the wardrobe closet, but solid, heavy, stompy boots. She loved them, and tears very nearly welled up in her eyes, though not quite. She placed them on the table and said, "These are great, guys."

"Top of the line. Those things will last you forever." Artie reached over and thumped one of them. "Steel toes, too. Once you enchant them and put some inertial magic on the toes? You'll be able to kick your way through reinforced concrete."

"This is the nicest thing anyone's ever given me," she said, and it was true.

"You'll need them. Starting tomorrow, you're going to be out in the field with Daniel and Jenny, and kicking stuff will probably enter into it. All this stuff before, it's just been practice. Now you're going to *work*."

"There's nothing I want more," she said, and that was true, too. Or mostly.

Late that night, after laying in bed for a while and considering the wisdom of acting on impulse, Marla slipped into the hallway and went to the room three doors down. She touched the knob, and it was unlocked; pushed it inward, and saw Daniel's sleeping form in the bed, his back to her, the room faintly illuminated by streaks of moonlight through the windowblinds.

She engaged the lock behind her.

Marla wore only a long t-shirt, and as she approached the bed she slipped it over her head and let it fall to the floor. She climbed into bed, under the covers, and when Daniel woke up and turned over—already glowing green and marshaling his powers, alert as they all were to possible danger—she covered his mouth with hers and kissed him the way she'd wanted to for months.

The green glow vanished. "You're... *naked*," he said, when their kiss broke.

"You're perceptive as always. And why aren't you naked?"

"Give me five seconds," he said, but didn't move. "Marla... not that I'm not happy to see you—and feel you—but you said you weren't interested. What changed?"

"I didn't say I wasn't interested, exactly." She ran her hands down his back, felt the muscles there—he was less scrawny than he'd been before Lao Tsung started making him work out. "Before, when I was just a trainee, on probation, whatever, it wouldn't have been right to do this. You were *teaching* me, there was this power imbalance..." She shook her head in the dark. "I wouldn't have been able to relax."

"But since we're equals now, you passed your test—you can relax?"

"I can. But maybe you should focus on getting me excited instead? You don't want me to get so relaxed I fall asleep."

He had the good sense to stop talking then, and they moved together, and sometimes at cross-purposes, and fumbled, and gasped, and—as most everyone does—they figured it out. Marla wondered if this was his first time. It was hers, and it was neither as wonderful as she'd hoped, nor as bad as she'd feared.

There was definitely something there, and like everything else in her life, she was confident this, too, would improve greatly with practice.

Chapter Eight

MARLA CREPT out of Daniel's room around 4 a.m., and found Artie sitting cross-legged in the hall, reading a tattered copy of *National Geographic*—doubtless one of the issues with topless tribeswomen. "Ah, hell," she said.

Without looking up from his magazine, Artie said, "I'm a pornomancer, kid. You think I wouldn't notice it happening in my own house?" He raised his voice. "Daniel. Come out here!"

After some shuffling and rustling, Daniel emerged wrapped in a sheet. "Uh, hey Artie, we were just—"

"Making the beast with two backs," Artie said. "Bumping uglies. Riding the baloney pony. Filling the taco. Hiding the salami. Pearl diving. Shooting the rapids."

Marla glanced at Daniel, who was blushing. Marla wondered if she was. She tried not to squirm uncomfortably, but this was like listening to your dad tell dirty jokes.

Artie kept up his euphemistic soliloquy. "Pinning the butterfly. Doing the two-bear mambo. Buttering the love muffin. Pulling the beef bus into tuna town. Conjugating the verb. Stuffing the ballot box."

"Okay, we get—" Daniel began, but Artie just spoke louder.

"Dipping the wick. Laying pipe. Breaking off a piece. Feeding the kitty. Boinking. Cream cheesing the bagel. Greasing the weasel. The horizontal mambo. Romancing the bone. Fucking." Now he looked at them. "You know why there are so many different ways of saying what you two did? Because human beings are obsessed with it. It's both the most common and the most sacred act in the world. The basic human needs are food, shelter, and security, but people will give up all of those in order to get at sex. It can wreck families and bring down careers and topple empires—and it can also make life worth living. Once you're sexually mature, for most folks, fucking is the secret puppetmaster lurking in your brain, the hormonal hijacker, the reason for intellectual rationalization and desperate excuses. Do I mind you two are fucking? No. Not inherently. But I have a question: Were you careful? And I don't mean about each other's feelings or avoiding unsightly bruising."

"This is your house, Artie," Marla said. "There are condoms all over." Along with other things, the precise uses of which sometimes eluded her, though she was sure she'd figure them out. "We were safe. I've got no intention of getting pregnant."

"I can also, ah, sap the life out of my... you know." Daniel gestured vaguely downward. "My swimmers. Like... magical spermicide."

Marla wrinkled her nose at that, but didn't speak.

"Okay," Artie said, "but don't rely on the magic. You'll only know if that's really working the time it *doesn't* work. Put your faith in latex, I always say. Now I've got a command." He stood up, and once again Marla saw past his schlubby persona to the steel and will underneath. "Do not let this screw up your work. If I see your studies slipping, I'll separate you, and I mean I'll put an *ocean* between you. And if you get goo-goo-eyed at each other in the field, you'll probably die, so I won't need to punish you then. And I know right now you probably think this is the one true forever love—"

Both Marla and Daniel started to make sounds of protest, but he bulldozed over them.

"But if you two decide to stop banging each other like screen doors, don't let it mess up your teamwork." He sighed. "Though that's probably me telling water to run uphill. This could make you work better together, improve your rapport, and I'll hope for that outcome. You hear me?"

They both nodded.

"And if you two do make a going concern of this... keep it quiet. I've got enemies, which means you do, too, and if those people find out you care for each other, they'll try to use one of you against the other. Keep the public displays of affection to nil. But, with those caveats: enjoy." He shook his head. "Gods, to be seventeen again, when you think you invented sex. Hell. Because you *did*. Everybody invents it every time. I'm so jealous of you two, you can't imagine. Go back to bed. The day starts in a couple of hours." He tromped off down the hall.

After a moment, Daniel said, "So, I guess you don't have to sneak back to your room now, huh?"

"And it's still two hours until breakfast," Marla said, and slapped his ass through the sheet.

They had an all-hands meeting scheduled for the afternoon at some bar south of the river—the first such meeting Marla had been invited to—but that wasn't for a few hours. Daniel was out doing the shopping, as he was still the de facto cook, and Marla went out onto the lowest deck in the house, the one close enough that you could sometimes feel the spray of the bay hitting rocks when the tide was in. The weather was glorious, the heat cut by the wind off the water, the view breathtakingly devoid of boats, nothing in view but the sparkle of the water.

Marla, who'd grown up in a doublewide trailer, felt a little thrill every time she stepped through the sliding glass doors and into this view.

Jenny Click sat in a chair with her feet up on the railing, reading a fat paperback novel. Her blonde hair blew back from her head and fluttered in the wind, and she wore a short white dress and oversized sunglasses, and Marla figured she could pass for a goddess, even without her halo of flame. *But I'm the one who got laid last night,* she though, and felt a little better.

She dragged a chair over closer to Jenny and put her own feet up. The two hadn't spent as much time together as Marla would have liked. Jenny was usually out doing Artie's business, whatever that was, but the times they did spend together were some of Marla's favorites, without any of the sparring tension or one-upmanship that sometimes sparked between her and Daniel.

"Marla," Jenny said, lowering her sunglasses. "You're *smiling.* I don't think I've seen you smile once before—the occasional nasty grin right before you knock me over in martial arts class, maybe, but not plain old *happy.*"

"Sometimes life is good," Marla said, suddenly embarrassed, looking down. "I mean, I passed my apprenticeship test…"

"It's more than that." Jenny reached over and touched Marla's chin, tipping her face up to look into her eyes. "You and Daniel finally quit your weird passive-aggressive version of flirting and just *did* it, didn't you?"

"Last night," Marla said, pride and shame warring within her, and all that topped with annoyance at herself for feeling such clichés of emotion.

"Your first time?"

Marla glanced around—like somebody could have sneaked up on them—and nodded. "Yeah. I mean, I've done stuff, back home when I was still in school, but it was the first time I've done... all of it."

"Stand up," Jenny said, rising, and Marla did. Jenny put her arms around her and hugged, and Marla hugged back, thinking that, even though Jenny was barely a year older than her, she was like an older sister, still—worldly and full of wisdom. Jenny released her and said "You are a woman now" in a deep and serious voice, and they both started laughing. They sat back down again. "Did Artie give you hell?"

"A little bit. How'd you know he knew?"

"He's Artie. I think he can tell when fish are fucking in the water under the deck. Daniel's been into you for a while, Marla. I hope things work out for you two. I don't know a lot about Daniel's past—Artie does, but he's good at keeping secrets when they matter—but he's got some demons. Be careful with him?"

I've got demons too, Marla thought, but said, "Don't worry. We'll be careful with each other. I think... we can help each other. It's sweet, though, you being worried about him. He cares about you, you know. He told me you're like a sister to him."

"That means a lot," Jenny said, and then they both sat in silence and looked at the ocean, Marla's mind running over the night before in pleasurable reminiscence, and Jenny doubtless thinking thoughts Marla could not divine.

Ernesto arrived late afternoon in a wheezing dirt-colored pickup truck, and Jenny and Marla squeezed in tight beside him, Jenny in the middle. Ernesto drove south of the river to a cruddy neighborhood full of check-cashing places and corner convenience stores, the kind of area where even the fast-food restaurants had bars on the windows. They were meeting Artie and Daniel at a place called Juliana's, which was almost entirely unremarkable, just an unlit sign and a door in a windowless gray wall. Ernesto knocked a complicated rhythm on the metal front door and it popped open of its own accord. "Ladies first," he said.

"We're not ladies, but okay." Jenny led the way into the club. There was a bar off to one side, and a dance floor, and it was all sort of forlorn and dirty-looking with the houselights on.

"Hey Juliana," Jenny said, waving toward the bar, where the proprietor leaned. She had short carroty hair, skin as pale and unhealthy-looking as weevily flour, and bags under her eyes so heavy they looked painted on with stage makeup.

Jenny angled away toward the dancefloor, and Marla followed, whispering, "Is that woman okay?"

"Don't know. She's always looked like that, every time I've seen her, like a junkie halfway through detox. Artie says the rumor is she's an addict, but nobody's sure what she's addicted to—something magical that's killing her really slowly, maybe, or maybe something she's been using so long she needs it to stay alive." Jenny shrugged. "She was supposed to be a pretty hot young sorcerer in her day, but now she's only important because she runs this place."

"And what's so important about this place?"

"That," Ernesto said, drawing up alongside her and pointing at a door that Marla had assumed led to a closet. He stepped forward and performed another complex knock—a different one, this time—and the door popped open.

Revealing a closet. Mop in a bucket, couple of brooms, shelves of cleaning supplies and toilet paper.

"In we go," Jenny said, and stepped inside. She passed through the mops and shelves as if they were fog, and disappeared from sight.

"Ah," Marla said. "It's like that." She went into the closet, willing herself not to flinch or try to step over the bucket, just striding through like Jenny had, and apart from a faint chill and a whiff of acetone, walking through the illusion was much like walking through air.

Beyond was a small conference room with a rectangular table and a few wheeled officechairs beneath an incongruous low-hanging pool-hall light. Artie sat in a chair at the head of the table, Daniel seated on his right. Artie gestured and said, "Sit, let's talk."

Marla hesitated for a moment—should she sit next to Daniel? Across from him? As far away as possible?—then decided she was being dumb and sat at the foot of the table facing Artie. Ernesto and Jenny took seats of their own, and Artie leaned forward, resting his elbows on the table and lacing his fingers together. "Welcome to the most valuable room in town."

Marla looked around. The room didn't look like much. It looked like a storeroom with a table jammed into it. "How's that?"

"This spot, where this room was built, nullifies magic. Nobody knows why. You can't work spells in here. And it's, like, insulated. A telepath standing right outside the door can't hear the thoughts of someone inside. Same with clairvoyance, clairaudience, hell, clair-smelling. None of it can penetrate this space. So it's the safest place in the city—on this coast—for sorcerers to have meetings in secret, or for guys who hate each other to meet without fear of killing each other. Magically, anyway." He nodded toward the door. "Sorcerers paying rent to use this place, that's what keeps Juliana out there comfortable."

"Okay." Marla glanced around at the others, who looked bored, presumably having heard all this before. "So why are we here? What's so secret?"

"Let me fill you in on the background real quick. I've got… let's call him a rival. I'd call him an enemy, but we're not quite at the point of setting each other's houses on fire. If I saw him at a party, we'd be polite to each other, you know? But we've got some conflicting interests. Namely, this." He snapped his fingers, and Daniel passed over a roughly cylindrical object about ten inches long. "Take a look." Artie rolled the thing down the table to Marla, who caught it before it could hit her in the chest. She turned it over and examined it.

"This is a penis made of rock," Marla said. "Are you guys hazing me? Is this a gag gift?" Even as she spoke, she knew it wasn't. The stone was oddly warm, and the sinuous carvings along its reddish-black shaft squirmed when she tried to examine them.

"It's an artifact, Marla. Incalculably old, incredibly powerful, and nobody knows if it was made by a sorcerer or dropped by a passing god or if it just sprang into existence spontaneously. Sacred stone phalli aren't that uncommon—they appear in lots of cultures, there's even a Festival of the Steel Phallus that still happens in Japan, but this… this is different."

Marla stared at the thing, and it occurred to her that the stone phallus was heavier than it should have been, and that as she looked at it, she had the oddest feeling it was looking back. "What does it do?"

"It's… unpredictable. Let's just say you wouldn't want to use it as a sex toy—it might impregnate you with a demon baby, or turn you into a man, or give you visions… same thing if a man slipped it into one of his orifices, though demon pregnancies are harder on men."

Marla put the thing down on the table, resting upright on its flattened base, mushroom-flared head pointed upward. "Doesn't sound like it's much good, Artie. I mean, it's pretty, and it's weird, but… it's not useful."

"That's because it's broken," Artie said. "It's half an artifact. There's a stone yoni—a symbolic vagina, though it doesn't look much like a vagina, really. An intricately carved curving thing, that that phallus fits into, like the pedestal of a statue. Only when the two pieces are combined is the artifact whole, and an object of greater power."

"What power's that?"

Artie smiled, his face oddly shadowed by the hanging light. "The power of immortality, kid. How'd you like to live forever?"

Marla thought about it. The possibility of her own death had never seemed very close, even in her desperate homeless days. But, practically, she knew the day would come, and she didn't think she would welcome it. She'd read enough cautionary fantasies to hedge her response, though: "I guess it would be okay, as long as you didn't age too much, or lose your mind."

Artie nodded. "That's it exactly. There are ways to live forever—well, we say forever, but what does that mean? Immortality just means you haven't died *yet*, and don't expect to—who knows what happens if you stick along until, say, the heat death of the universe? But eventually, after enough centuries, all the sorcerers who've extended their lives start to go crazy. I don't just mean they forget what it's like to be human, start to view everybody else as no more important than beetles—hell, less important than dust mites. That happens, too. But I mean *crazy*. They become monstrous. They see things that aren't there—or maybe things that are there, that you can't see unless you've lived five thousand years. They behave erratically. They start to remember the future and forget the past. And, eventually, they kill themselves, or other people kill them, or if they *can't* die, they find a way to sleep. And we all hope they'll never wake up." He pointed at the statue. "But the stories say, if you use this artifact, you can maintain your humanity and sanity forever—that you can become, pretty much, like a god. Sounds good, huh?"

"It does," Marla said.

"Glad you think so. Because we're probably going to have to kill this motherfucker to get it." He slid a photograph to Daniel, who passed it to Jenny, who passed it to Marla. It was a black-and-white headshot of an older, handsome man with a strong nose and white hair swept back dramatically from his forehead. He had the kind of profile that belonged on coins. "Clive Rasmussen," Artie said. "A big-shot English sorcerer, though he's been hanging out in the states entirely too much for my taste lately. We've been going back and forth for years, each of us offering to buy the other's half of the artifact, never coming to an agreement. But he's up to something now, and I want to know what. Especially since he sent somebody to my town to steal something from right underneath my nose."

"The librarian at the Catholic school, the one Artie sent me to investigate?" Jenny said. "We're pretty sure he was working for Rasmussen." She touched her forehead. "I caught him trying to steal a book, and he cracked me on the head, but…" She shook her head. "He didn't get away."

"He's just a soot stain on concrete now," Artie said, "and *I've* got the book. Not that I know what good it is. It's an old travelogue from an 18th-century naturalist, mostly about some megalithic ruins down in the Pacific islands, in Micronesia. Basically a whole artificial city built who knows how long ago, these huge basalt slabs rising out of the ocean. I dunno what Rasmussen wants with that place, but I'm gonna find out."

"Why don't you two just, I don't know, cooperate?" Marla said. "Bring your halves of the artifact together so you can both be immortal?"

"No way," Artie said. "Having that son of a bitch around for eternity would totally spoil my enjoyment of forever. But I am arranging a meeting with him, to sell him this book, after making a copy of my own, of course. We're getting together in a couple of days, in this very room, each of us bringing just one apprentice to help with security. And you, Marla, are going to be my apprentice. Think you can stand around and look menacing?"

Marla shrugged. She didn't care much about looking menacing. She just wanted to be capable of causing mayhem. "Sure. I guess you want me there because magic doesn't work in this room, and I'm better at breaking faces without magic?"

"There's that," Artie said. "But Daniel, Ernesto, and Jenny are going to be busy, breaking into Rasmussen's mansion while he's here in faraway Felport."

Marla laughed. "So they're going to steal the artifact?"

Artie shook his head. "I doubt *that*. If they happen to see it lying around, sure, but he's probably got it under locks and keys like you can't imagine. They're mostly going on an information-gathering mission to rifle through his office and figure out what he's got planned. Maybe it doesn't have anything to do with me, but right now, Rasmussen and I are pretty evenly matched, and I don't want him getting any more powerful—not powerful enough to knock me down and take my stuff, anyway. Getting the other half of the artifact… that's the ultimate goal, but we're playing a long game, and I don't expect to win this year or even necessarily this decade. When the stakes are immortality, I can be patient."

The rest of the meeting was given over to blueprints and logistics and poring over documents for the part of the plan that had nothing to do with Marla, but she paid attention anyway, because it was better to know things than not. When they were done, Artie tossed her the keys to the Bentley. "Me and Ernesto gotta go visit a guy. You drive home. Don't wait dinner—I'll be back late."

After they departed, Jenny said, "You guys want to have some fun? Maybe hit the boardwalk, eat some fried dough, enjoy the last dribs and drabs of summer?"

Marla glanced at Daniel, wondering if he was thinking what she was. "That sounds fun," Marla said, "but you guys are flying off to England tomorrow, and, uh…"

"We thought maybe, you know, we might spend a little time together, the two of us…" Daniel said, reaching over and putting his hand on Marla's shoulder.

"Fucking like greased bunnies?" Jenny said. She rolled her eyes. "Fine. I'll make my own way home. More fried dough for me."

After Jenny left, Daniel moved his hand somewhere a bit more interesting than Marla's shoulder and said, "How fast do you think you can get us home and into bed?"

"Why go home first? The Bentley's got a big back seat."

"I like the way you think. I wish you were going to England with me."

"Me too. Just don't get eaten by a guard dog, okay? I want you to come back to me."

"I'll always come back, as long as you're what's waiting for me," he said.

Chapter Nine

MARLA SAT CLEANING HER FINGERNAILS with a throwing knife, tipped back in her chair in the corner of the conference room facing the door, smacking chewing gum. Playing thug. She was having the time of her life.

Rasmussen came into the room trailed by his own apprentice, a weaselly-faced red-haired man who seemed more a collection of tics and tremors than a person. "Mann," Rasmussen said, nodding to Artie before sitting down on the other side of the table. His apprentice looked at Marla, snorted laughter, and leaned back against the wall, crossing his arms. Marla was serene. She could throw her knife into his eye if she wanted to, and that knowledge bred serenity. Well, she'd hit the eye three times out of five, anyway. Lao Tsung said she still needed more practice.

"Finding your apprentices at junior high schools now?" Rasmussen said.

"Better than scraping them off the bottom of my shoe," Artie replied. "How you doing, you Limey fuck?"

"The world continues to unveil itself for me, Arthur."

"My first name is Artemis, you asshole."

"Ah, yes, I should have remembered, you were named after a goddess—fitting, for a cockless anomaly like yourself." He sighed. "I relish these little conversations less and less as time goes on, dear Diana. Let's do our business and be done, shall we?"

Artie snapped his fingers, and Marla leaned forward to hand him the book, never taking her eyes off the weaselly apprentice, in case he tried to take advantage of a moment's distraction. He didn't pay her any attention, and she resumed her post.

"Interesting reading," Artie said, tapping the book's worn cover.

"Mmm," Rasmussen said. "Here's a check for the amount we agreed on." He slid a slip of paper across the table.

"You're taking a personal check?" Marla blurted, and Artie turned to give her the most vicious look she'd ever seen from him. "I just mean—"

"Shut up," Artie said, and turned back to Rasmussen, who was chuckling to himself. "Here." He shoved the book hard, and it skidded toward Rasmussen's waiting fingers. The English sorcerer handed the book over his shoulder to his apprentice, who tucked it out of sight.

"I assume you made a copy?" Rasmussen said.

"Sure," Artie said.

"Shame it won't do you any good. The information I want is written in heat-sensitive invisible ink. Don't suppose you had the sense to hold the end papers over a candle flame?"

"You're lying," Artie said. "You're fucking with me."

"No, I daresay I'm done fucking with you, Artie. I never want to see or speak to you again."

Artie snorted. "Sure, sell me your half of the artifact, and I'll be happy to—"

"No." Rasmussen shook his head. "I'm done trying to strike that sort of bargain, too. My interest in you has utterly departed. I don't care about your little stone cock anymore. You should keep it. After all, you don't want to be *entirely* dickless, do you?" He rose, nodded to Marla gravely, and departed, followed by his jittery apprentice.

Artie turned on her. "Did I tell you to *talk*?"

Marla shrank back. Artie occasionally gave her shit, but she'd seldom seen him actually pissed. "No, but come on, a personal check? From your sworn enemy? I mean—"

"To a guy like that, Marla, money is nothing. Money is easy. He can always get more. There's no *reason* he'd stop the check, or write it on a non-existent account, because he doesn't *care*. By speaking out like you did, you made it seem like I'm the kind of schmuck who *does* care about money, like I'm less successful than him, like..." He shook his head. "*Fuck.* That went badly. I can't believe he was telling the truth about invisible ink. I figured there was maybe a cipher, a code, I've got guys working on breaking it, but if that's true... And what did he mean about not caring about my half of the artifact? It's got to be a head-fake, he's going to pretend he doesn't want it anymore, then offer to... No. I don't get it. But he's up to something." Artie chewed his lower lip, deep in thought.

After a moment, Marla cleared her throat. "I'm really sorry, Artie."

He waved her away. "It's okay, kid. I shoulda told you to keep mum. I'm just preoccupied."

"Maybe Jenny and Daniel and Ernesto will come up with some info after they raid his house."

"Let's hope so. Because right now I feel like I'm playing chess when all along I thought I was playing checkers."

"Nothing," Daniel said again, shaking his head and pointing to the glossy photographs on the table. "Big map of some Pacific islands on the wall. A whiteboard with all these symbols—we don't know what they are—but the numbers are latiitudes and longitudes and depths, all mostly just spots in the middle of the ocean."

"But *nothing* about me?" Artie leaned over the dining room table. "Not a mention of my name, nothing about Felport, nothing about my half of the artifact?"

Ernesto and Jenny exchanged glances. Ernesto cleared his throat. "We went through his trash. Found a big thick file with your name on it. But the contents had been shredded."

"Did you bring the pieces back?" Artie said. "Find out what he's trying to hide?"

"The shreds were ruined, Artie," Jenny said. "They were in the garbage. There was… garbage juice soaking them. Leaky Chinese food containers, rotting fruit, stuff like that."

"And what do you mean 'trying to hide'?" Ernesto said. "Hide from who? He threw it away. There was no attempt at hiding it. It's not like he shredded those files special—all his thrown-out papers were shredded, even the junk mail, I think he just has his apprentices do it as a matter of course."

"Rasmussen did say he was over the whole vendetta thing," Marla said. "I mean… maybe he was telling the truth. The stuff on the walls, the book, is does seem like he's got a different obsession now."

Artie leaned back and scowled at her. "Marla. I have half an artifact that can grant him immortality. You think he's just gonna… get over that? No way. He must have known you were coming or something, he faked up that stuff in the trash—"

"Yeah, *that's* the most logical explanation." Ernesto shook his head, a look of profound disgust on his face.

"You, my office, *now*." Artie pointed at Ernesto, then stomped off out of the room.

Ernesto sighed heavily. "See you guys later. Dad has to yell at me now."

They sat for a moment, hearing Artie's voice raised, and Ernesto's raised in return, until Daniel said, "How about we get the fuck out of here? I just spent three days eating English food. I could use a real cheeseburger."

"God, that blood sausage," Jenny said. "I thought you were going to puke when they put it on the table."

"What about you—what did you think a shepherd's pie *was*? Did you think it was made of actual shepherds?"

Marla felt a flash of jealousy—Jenny and Daniel had spent time together, they'd bonded, they had private jokes, and she felt suddenly, intensely, left out. So she went to Daniel, insinuated herself into his lap, and said, "I thought you didn't even need to eat?"

Daniel put his arms around her waist, but entirely too absent-mindedly for Marla's taste. "Well, sure, I can sustain myself by drawing on the life-energy around me, but I still *like* to eat. Food is yum."

"And here I thought I was lucky enough to find a man who could live on love alone," Marla said. And wiggled, just a little, in his lap.

"Ah," Daniel said, looking away from Jenny, at last. "I guess maybe not love *alone*."

"Love and sex alone?" Marla said.

"Guys. I'm sitting right here," Jenny said.

"Right," Daniel said. "I guess we should go someplace... more private then."

"You two are ridiculous," Jenny said. "It would be cute if I wasn't choking on my own puke. I'll see you both for dinner?"

"If we're done by then," Marla said.

"I am a shallow jealous bitch," Marla said, hours later, in Jenny's room. Marla'd had fun with Daniel, certainly, but afterward she'd thought of Jenny, jetlagged and probably lonely, and marveled at her own capacity for pettiness. So here she was.

Jenny was on her bed, painting her toenails fire-engine red. "Daniel's all yours, Marla. Really. He couldn't stop talking about you on the trip, saying he wished you could've seen this or if only you could have heard that." She pulled her foot up close to her lips—Marla was just as flexible, but Jenny managed to look graceful doing it—and blew on the wet toenails. "It would be dumb for us to let a boy get between us, especially when he pretty much thinks of me as a sister." She looked up. "But a sister *is* close, Marla. Do you really want Daniel to stop hanging out with me?"

"No," Marla said. "I just missed him. And I guess… I can get territorial. Probably because of how I was raised."

"Probably. Come here. Let me paint your nails."

Marla looked down at her steel-toed boots and thought of her sweaty feet inside. She hadn't painted her toenails since junior high. "Seriously?"

"Get over here before I decide I should braid your hair, too."

Artie brooded. He spent long hours in his office, yelling on the phone, and poring over the non-erotic books in his library (they were kept in a secret room, which actually had a bookshelf for a door, like something from a story). He paced, and mumbled, and whenever Ernesto came over they yelled at each other behind closed doors. Dinners were a rather strained affair, and the apprentices were all glad that half the time Artie never even came to the table.

He didn't send them out on missions, either, which gave them all rare and blessed free time. Marla and Jenny and Daniel just tried to stay clear of Artie's wrath, and spent as much time as possible out in the city, enjoying the last of the warm weather. They all spent a lot of time studying, too, with Lao Tsung—who had a nasty cough lately, though the cold didn't seem to slow him down at all—and pursuing their own magical studies, practicing in the real world or Artie's London, honing their skills through overlearning. Marla spent most nights in Daniel's bed. Apart from their boss's crankiness, it was a golden time.

About a month after the meeting with Rasmussen, Artie called them together. "I've been a shitty teacher. I'm sorry about that. I've been trying to figure out what the Limey bastard's got planned, and that's important, but I shouldn't neglect you three. So I'm gonna make it up to you. There's a council meeting tonight. I'm taking you all with me."

"Whoa," Daniel said. "I thought Ernesto usually went with you?"

Artie closed his eyes, briefly. "Maybe don't say his name today, okay? We're having… a difference of opinion. I'm not too happy with him. Meeting's at sunset. You three dress nice. Don't make me look bad. See you then." He went back to his office and shut the door.

"Awesome," Daniel said. "We finally get to meet Sauvage, Cochran, Sorenson, the Chamberlain, the Bay Witch…"

"So this is, like, a meeting of all the sorcerers?" Marla said. She had only the vaguest understanding of the city's magical organization, except that Artie was pretty well up in the hierarchy, but not at the top.

"Yeah." Jenny nodded. "They don't meet often, maybe once a year I guess, unless there's some big emergency. It's like… a meeting of the Five Families from *The Godfather* or something. I've never been to one, but Ernesto's told us about them."

"Should be interesting," Marla said.

Except it wasn't that interesting, at first. The meeting was in a sparsely, but elegantly, furnished penthouse apartment belonging to one of the sorcerers, a bald black man named Hamil. Their group was among the first to arrive, and Artie went straight to eating canapes and talking to a group that included Hamil, a slim Asian man, an old white guy with a nose big as a cowcatcher, and a gorgeous blonde woman with wet hair. The apprentices drifted toward a knot of other younger people by the windows.

A serious-faced, dark-haired young man, maybe in his mid-twenties, turned and looked them up and down. "Ah," he said. "You must be Mann's brood."

" I guess so," Marla said, and he nodded with exaggerated dignity.

"I am Gregor, Mr. Cochran's protégé. I am studying the ways of divination."

"Huh. I'm Marla. I mostly break stuff. This is Jenny—she mostly burns stuff."

"We've met before," Jenny said, voice unusually frosty, and turned away to talk to another apprentice.

"Uh," Marla said. "And this is Daniel."

"Ah, the Breatharian," Gregor said, with the ghost of a smile.

"What's a Breatharian?"

"Crazy idiots who die of starvation," Daniel said. "Or else liars. Mostly con artists who claim they can teach people Inedia—the ability to live on spiritual energy alone, with no need for food or drink, just air. They say they can live on light."

"But you *can* live on light," Gregor said. "Correct?"

"I can live on *prana*, anyway," he said. "But Breatharians *can't*, and they steal money from gullible people who think they can. Don't call me one of them. It's like calling you, I don't know, a storefront fortune teller."

"Mmm. You're overly sensitive. How interesting. I can tell you belong to Artie."

"We don't belong to anybody—" Marla began, but Gregor turned and walked away as if she hadn't spoken at all.

"That guy sucks," Marla said, and Daniel didn't disagree.

More sorcerers arrived, including a beautiful black woman in a shimmering evening gown, a leggy blonde dressed all in white with a smile so icy you could practically scrape frost off it, and some more middle-aged white men. Jenny and Daniel pointed out the ones they knew. The black woman was called the Chamberlain, and had something to do with ghosts; the blonde was Susan Wellstone, master of long-form ritual magic (Marla made a note to try to talk to her—she was interested in that kind of stuff); and the damp blonde was the Bay Witch, by all accounts a strange personality.

Marla and Daniel mingled with the other apprentices, careful not to show one another any particular affection, and to keep appearances businesslike. Jenny mostly talked to a scarred bald guy named Partridge, apparently sharing tips on pyromancy. The big room gradually filled up, with the city's leading sorcerers taking chairs while their retinues lined the edges of the room. Finally, after they'd been there nearly an hour, the front door banged open and a man walked in alone.

He was big, and fat, but unlike Artie's softness, his was a hard sort of fat, fat over muscle, and he moved with the self-assurance of a professional athlete. He wore a nice gray suit and a big ruby pinky ring, and though his hair was thinning and going gray, his eyes were sharp and searching. This had to be Sauvage, Marla thought. Felport's chief sorcerer. Artie talked about him like he'd hung the moon. No, like he could beat the *shit* out of the moon. Like he could eat the moon and crap out the tides afterward.

Sauvage slapped backs and shook hands and whispered into ears, making a personal connection with everybody—except the guy with the cowcatcher nose, Gregor's boss, Cochran. He eyed Sauvage warily, and got ignored in return. After the gladhanding, Sauvage took the biggest chair in the room, laced his hands over his belly, and said, "So that's everybody, right? Wait, where the fuck is Viscarro?"

A quivering apprentice wearing a white shirt and a pocket protector stepped forward, clutching a little notebook. "My master sends his regrets, and asked me to take notes—"

"Why am I not shocked?" Sauvage, voice booming. "Fuck it, Viscarro doesn't get a vote, then. The rest of you—what are we going to do about this plague of fucking angels?"

Marla glanced at Jenny and Daniel, who both shrugged. They hadn't heard anything about angels either, apparently.

"We should continue to consult the oracles and auguries—" Cochran said, and Sauvage waved him away.

"I knew what *you'd* say—wait and see, wait and see. Eventually you gotta do something, Cochran. These things, these Thrones, they're starting to piss me off. Showing up at places that are supposed to be private, making threats about judgment and consequences. What the fuck are they?"

"Maybe they're angels," the Bay Witch said. "Why shouldn't things be what they say they are?" She then lowered her head and lapped at the punchbowl like a dog drinking from a water dish, which diminished the force of her argument somewhat, Marla thought.

"I don't believe in angels," the Asian guy—whose name was Sorenson, unlikely as that seemed—said. "Maybe they *think* they're angels, but messengers from god? Which god? I don't buy it."

"That Limey sorcerer, Rasmussen," Artie said. "Maybe he's behind it, trying to fuck with our heads—"

"Gods, Artie," Sauvage said, clutching his head. "Again with the Englishman! I know you guys are in a pissing contest, but just because your life revolves around him doesn't mean the rest of us give a shit, okay? I *know* Rasmussen, and he knows me, and this isn't his kind of thing." He looked around the room. "Has anybody caught one of these Thrones? Let's get one. Interrogate it. Cut it up and see how it works if we've gotta. Find out what—"

There was a crackle and a smell like a burned-out power transformer, and a man appeared in the center of the room. He looked like a wino with his untucked flannel shirt, stubbly face, and stained pants, but pale light leaked from the corners of his eyes, and his hair drifted about as if charged with static electricity. He looked around, and as his head turned, eyes appeared briefly in his cheeks, his throat, and his forehead, opening for a moment, then closing and vanishing. "Sorcerers," he said, and his voice was high-pitched, almost songlike, almost pretty. "We are Thrones. We watch. We note your crimes. We compile the lists. There will come a judgment. Consider your actions. Consider the consequences. The consequences of eternity. Consider—"

"Get him!" Sauvage shouted, and Marla—who'd been waiting for the order, on some level—launched herself past the staring sorcerers, first in a crowd of surging apprentices. In the edges of her vision Marla saw Jenny rising in her aura of flame, and Daniel reaching out with his hands, a quizzical look on his face, but the main focus of her attention was on the creature who called himself a Throne. She got to him first and delivered a roundhouse kick, the steel-toed boots whipping into his guts—

—and she spun around uselessly. She might as well have kicked a sheet hanging on a clothesline, and indeed, only a mound of stinking clothes remained where he'd been. "He disappeared," she said.

"I noticed. Good try, though." Sauvage stood up. "She one of yours, Artie?"

"Yeah," he said, pride unmistakable in his voice.

"Good," Sauvage said, never looking at Marla. He prodded the Throne's discarded clothing with his toe. "Somebody want to get these analyzed? Maybe that guy, what's his name, Langford? The freelancer? Get him to look at this stuff."

"The Throne," Daniel said, and everyone turned to look at him, most of the sorcerers obviously irritated at his interruption. Daniel blushed at the attention, but kept going. "I can sense life, you know, life-force, and… there wasn't life there. Whatever the Throne was, it's not alive, not like anything else I've ever seen."

"It wasn't a ghost," the Chamberlain said.

"Or an illusion of any kind," Sorenson added.

"Nothing from out of nature at all," said a hulking, confused-looking guy with dirt on his face. Granger, his name was, some kind of nature magician.

"Huh," Sauvage said. "Maybe it is an angel then." He looked around. "So your homework assignment is: how the fuck do we kill some angels?"

"That thing was freaky," Daniel said, lying in bed with Marla that night.

She rested her head on his chest. "The Throne? Yeah. Weirdest thing I've ever seen. And I've—"

"Seen Artie with his pants off, yes, I know, ha ha. But seriously… you really think those things are watching us? All the time?"

"Who knows?" Marla said. "But if they are, how about we give them a show?"

They passed the night pleasantly, and slept, until Artie pounded on the bedroom door just before dawn. "Come on," he shouted. "Down to the basement, now, now, now!"

They got out of bed, struggling into clothes, and Daniel said, "Is something wrong? Are we under attack?"

"No!" Artie yelled. "That fucker Ernesto's abandoning us, so we've got to break the geas. He's leaving the family. He's *dead* to me, and if he dies, I don't want to be on the hook for avenging him. Come on. I want this bullshit over with by breakfast. I'll be damned if I'll let that ingrateful piece of shit spoil my whole day." He stormed away.

"Shit," Daniel said. "I knew they were fighting, but... leaving the family?"

"Yeah," Marla said, quietly. Thinking of her own original family. Thinking: *Why did I ever think this one would be any better at lasting forever?*

They went downstairs, to help Artie and Ernesto break all their promises to one another.

Chapter Ten

THE RITUAL TO BREAK Ernesto's connection to Artie's little family was much the same as the ritual that had included him, only this time, Ernesto stepped out of the chalked circle, and Artie scuffed out the carefully-drawn lines with his heel. The hum of magic fled the room, and Marla stood very still, trying to tell whether or not she felt spiritually diminished, having lost one of the people who'd been sworn to protect and avenge her.

But she didn't feel much of anything, except sad.

Artie spat on the floor near Ernesto's feet. Marla didn't think that was part of the ritual. It seemed more like editorial spittle.

Ernesto walked over to where Jenny, Daniel, and Marla stood together in a hushed and slumped cluster. "Guys," he said. "I hope we can still be friends. My decision isn't any reflection on you. I just…" He glanced over his shoulder at Artie, who was still scuffing away at the chalk, staring furiously at the floor. "I don't agree with the way certain things are going. I decided it wasn't doing anybody any good if—"

"Get the fuck out of here," Artie said, looking up. "Don't try to poison their minds against me."

Ernesto sighed and shook his head. "It's not like that, Artie. I owe you, I respect you, and if you ever need me, you can call—but I don't want to be pledged to avenge you when you seem determined to launch a suicidal grudge-attack at a guy like Rasmussen. Especially when Rasmussen doesn't pose a threat to us anymore. It's like entrusting my safety to somebody who likes to juggle hand grenades, Artie—"

"You think you're so fucking smart," Artie said, closing the distance between himself and Ernesto, standing so close their chests were nearly touching. "You were just a stupid little nothing when I met you. I taught you everything you know, but you think you know *better* than me?"

"I'll always love you like a father, Artie," Ernesto said, voice touched with sadness. "But it's time for me to leave home."

"Get. The fuck. Out of my house."

"Goodbye, guys," Ernesto said, glancing back over his shoulder at his former-fellow apprentices. "I'll be staying at my cousin's junkyard if you need me."

"Nobody needs you. Go!" Artie drew back his fist, and Ernesto sighed.

"I'm going." And he went.

Artie watched Ernesto tromp up the stairs out of the basement, still with his arm cocked back, as if his former protégé might return for that punch to the face after all. Then Artie slumped. "I'm going to my office. You three... stay out of trouble." He departed.

Jenny hugged herself. "That was horrible. My family used to fight like that. I thought I was past all that." She looked at Marla. "Do you think... Ernesto's right? I mean, about Artie not being willing to let this thing with Rasmussen go?"

"Doesn't matter," Daniel said. "I owe Artie my life. Literally. I'd follow him to hell's front door and help him bust it down, if he wanted. Ernesto's a fucking ingrate. I'll see you two later. I've got some stuff I'm working on." He reached over and gave Marla's shoulder a squeeze, but his mind was clearly ten million miles away.

"What's he mean?" Marla said. "About owing Artie his life? He's never told me how they met, what happened, not really."

Jenny shook her head. "I'm not sure exactly. Artie's mentioned things, Daniel too, but I've never pieced it all together. And, you know, we all pretend to be people without a past around here. It seems impolite to dig into that old nasty stuff."

Marla nodded. She was certainly happy to leave her past back there behind her. "So what do we do now?"

"I was going to go flying," Jenny said. "Just get away for a while and think, you know?"

"Sure," Marla said. She knew how to fly, in theory, but it wasn't especially pleasant—it was more a barely-controlled fall away from conventional gravity than superhero-style soaring. But Jenny's power over flame and heat allowed her to hover and fly in a more elegant way, and a simple look-away spell kept the normals on the ground from noticing her. "I think I'll go see Lao Tsung, try to get a workout in. Beating up on the heavy bag always takes my mind off my problems."

But when she found Lao Tsung in his suite of rooms just off the gym, he was packing a bag. "Hey," she said. "What's up, tough guy?"

"Leaving town, killer," Lao Tsung said, crossing the room to his dresser, and pausing to plant a kiss on top of her head. "Going to San Francisco. Picture me with some flowers in my hair, huh?"

Marla frowned. Ernesto abandoning them was one thing, but Lao Tsung was leaving too? It wasn't like they ever had long heart-to-heart talks, but she felt as close to him as she did to Daniel and Jenny. She worked out with Lao almost every day, and they had a deep understanding of one another's capabilities, strengths, and weaknesses—they sparred, they conditioned, they learned to work in synch. Marla was pretty good at punching and kicking things, and Lao was the reason why. If she was honest, she was probably better at fighting than she was at magic, which maybe meant Lao was a better teacher than Artie. "Why? When are you coming back?"

"I think my work here is done, Marla. I could keep teaching you, sure—the kind of work we do, it's the work of a lifetime—but you've got the discipline now, you can study with others and I wouldn't worry about you. And Daniel and Jenny…" He shook his head and smiled. "Well, they do try, I made sure of that, but it's a good thing they can slurp out *qi* and make stuff explode by looking at it."

"So… that's it? You did your job and now you're leaving?" She sat down on the edge of her bed. Had she become so attached to someone who viewed her as simply a task to finish?

Lao sat down beside her. "Not… entirely. I've got cancer, Marla."

She frowned. "So go see a *bruja* and get it cured."

He laughed. "I've done that. I've done that *many* times. I've lived for a long time, Marla—not long enough to lose my humanity, but long enough that I worry about it a little, try to police myself, try to pay attention. I never did anything to make myself immortal, no rites or rituals or magic, I just… don't age. Never was sure why. Demi-god in my ancestry somewhere? Exposure to weird radiation when I was a kid? Did a favor for an angel in disguise and got this as a reward? Just got overlooked by death? Couldn't tell you. But the cancer, in my throat… it first popped up about forty years ago. I got it cured by magic, but it came back. Cured it again, came back again. Superficially unaging or not, this body of mine is old. Errors are creeping in. I'm sick of it."

"So you're going to San Francisco? Why? They got good acupuncture there?"

"Heh. Probably. But, no, they've got an artifact. It's called the Cornerstone, and it's supposed to keep the city from getting totally trashed in a big earthquake. The Cornerstone doesn't really do much, not on its own, but it's sort of a… binding agent. Most spells don't last forever, they decay, or fall apart when their creator stops maintaining them. Same goes for healing spells. But if you cast a spell with the help of the Cornerstone… it *does* last forever. So I'm gonna go and twist some arms and charm some folks until I find the Cornerstone, and I'm gonna get rid of this cancer for *good*."

Marla nodded. "And then… you'll come back?"

"Nothing I need to come back for, sweetie. And I'll probably owe about ten million favors out on the west coast by the time I'm through. But, I tell you what—you come out and visit me sometime, okay? And in the meantime, you can drive me to the airport, after I say goodbye to Artie."

When Marla returned from dropping Lao Tsung off at the airport, she followed the sounds of shouting to Artie's office, where he and Daniel were yelling at each other over Artie's ridiculously big desk. *Fuck*, she thought. *First Ernesto, now Daniel? Is there going to be anybody* left?

"What are you two screaming about?" she said.

They both turned and looked at her. "I'm trying to solve all Artie's problems, and he's tearing me a new asshole!"

"I like his old asshole just fine, Artie," Marla said. "What's going on?"

"This… this… this *moron* is messing with knowledge man was not meant to possess!" Artie said.

Marla blinked. "I thought forbidden knowledge was our whole thing?"

"Sure, okay, I phrased that wrong—he's messing with shit it's *dangerous* to know."

"I uncover the secret of immortality, and this is the response I get? I've spent months figuring this out!"

"Both of you, sit down," Marla said. "And tell me what you're talking about. Inside voices, please."

"Wants to play mediator," Artie muttered, but he sat in his executive swivel chair. Daniel, his expression a combination of sullenness and indignation, sat in one of the chairs on this side of the desk, and Marla joined him.

"Basically, I figured out how to live forever," Daniel said. "How to hook directly into *prana*, *qi*, and let it sustain you, lengthen your telomeres, keep your cells from undergoing screwy mutations—and I came to Artie to tell him he can stop worrying about that stupid artifact! *I* can make him live forever!"

"Living forever was never the problem," Artie said, but his anger had seemingly drained away. Now he just sounded tired. "There are half a dozen ways to extend life. Yeah, I'm impressed that you stumbled on this particular method independently, but it's old, too. Holy men like it. Mystics. But it's got a flaw—eventually, divorced from bodily concerns, you stop caring about the body. About the physical world entirely. You melt into *qi*, lose your sense of individuality, until eventually you drop your body like an old suit and just dissolve your consciousness into the universal life force like a spoonful of sugar dissolving into the ocean."

"Oh," Daniel said. "I... didn't know that."

Artie shrugged. "It's one of the better ways to go crazy by becoming immortal, I'll grant you that. Doesn't lead to psychotic breaks or deep delusions or world-destroying whims. Tell me you haven't done it, Daniel. That you haven't... connected yourself to *prana* that way."

Daniel shook his head. "I wasn't sure how, I was going to ask for your help... But no, I haven't."

Artie nodded. "Good." He leaned back in his chair, in control again, lacing his fingers across his belly. "The reason I want the other half of my artifact is to live forever without horrible consequences. Without melting into life-force slurry or going crazy. It's not the immortality—it's the *sanity*, the *humanity*, you see?"

"I don't really get it," Marla said. "The whole I'll-go-crazy-if-I-live-forever thing. I mean, Lao Tsung's been around a long time, and you're saying if he keeps living, he'll just... flip out one day?"

"It can be quick," Artie said. "Or it can be gradual. And, yeah, I hope Lao Tsung just turns out to be really long-lived and not actually immortal, because I don't want to see a friend turn into a monster. There's a place about an hour outside the city called the Blackwing Institute. It's where we put sorcerers who are too dangerous to live but too difficult to kill. There are only about a dozen inmates, some scarier than others, but two of the worst are immortals who have utterly lost their shit. One of them is named Norma Nilson—that's not her real name, it's just what she calls herself—and her craziness manifested as complete and total nihilism. She realized, after living about two thousand years, that nothing mattered, that the universe was just a blind clashing mechanistic place, and that consciousness in such a pointless world was the only true hell. She didn't even mean anybody harm, that's the funny thing—but she was such a powerful projecting empath that her total existential despair infected anyone who came within miles of her. A whole *town* in New England committed suicide when she passed through. I don't just mean the people. The *cows* slammed their heads into fenceposts until they bashed their brains in. Birds flew as high as they could and then just dropped. Fish jumped out of the water until they drowned in the air. You see what I'm saying? Some sorcerers knocked her unconscious with mortar shells and then we got her locked up in a nice insulated cell, where she can contemplate nothingness. Which is what she'll keep doing. *Forever.*"

"Doesn't make immortality sound so good," Marla said.

Artie shook his head. "And she's not the worst. Like I said, she doesn't have malice. Blackwing's most dangerous inmate is a woman named Elsie Jarrow. She was a chaos magician. She bound herself to the randomness of the universe. As long as chaos exists, she'll live, and since chaos is eternal, she's good until the whole universe cools off to absolute zero. But that chaos infected every part of her. She's only corporeal about one day in ten. Some days she's a cloud of toxic gas. Some days she's typhoid fever. Some days she's just electromagnetism. She's like a cancer with consciousness. It's not even possible to ascribe motivations to her, except for the desire to spread chaos, but the thing is, when she's human-looking, she *laughs*, and she makes threats. On some level, she knows what she's doing." He shook his head. "We keep her in a special cell deep underground, in steel and concrete, all bound up with magic based on order and math and pure patterns. Pray she never gets out." Artie opened a drawer in his desk and took out a bottle of small-batch bourbon. "And thinking about *that* dark and dismal shit makes me need a drink."

"Pour one for me while you're at it," Daniel said.

"You kids are underage," Artie said. "Go out and drink a milkshake or something wholesome instead. Enjoy being young enough that my obsession with immortality doesn't make any sense to you." He snorted. "Neither one of you is even twenty yet. Deep down inside you still think you're immortal *anyway*. Lucky little bastards." He shooed them away.

The next two years passed with relatively few disasters.

Lao Tsung sent them a postcard from San Francisco with a scrawled note saying, "Found what I needed, feeling fine," but didn't include a return address.

Artie bought a share in a porn video company and took numerous business trips to the west coast, though he didn't bother taking his apprentices with him, saying it was boring "if you aren't a dirty old man like me." If he remained obsessed with Rasmussen, he kept it relatively quiet.

Ernesto visited sometimes while Artie was out of town, bringing tidbits of gossip about the other sorcerers. He was doing a lot of work for Sorenson, the master illusionist, and seemed to be thriving. Marla, Jenny, and Daniel were divided on whether they envied him or not.

They all continued their studies. Jenny had flown as high as the troposphere. Daniel went three months straight without eating food or drinking water, living solely on the life force of the world, and broke his long fast with a feast that had them all sprawled around the house groaning for days. Marla continued to study the ass-kicking arts, and, with Artie's permission, started contracting out occasionally as a bodyguard and general muscle, helping Hamil to crack down on the half-wild gangs of apprentices and alley witches who warred on one another and threatened to reveal the existence of magic to the ordinaries.

Sometimes the Thrones appeared, crackling and making ominous pronouncements, but since they never *did* anything, most sorcerers started to consider them nothing but a nuisance, the supernatural equivalent of hungry pigeons.

There were occasional other missions and little intrigues, and two incidents where Sauvage, as chief sorcerer, called upon all the city's sorcerers to fight supernatural threats: once when a pack of spectral black dogs appeared in the city, their howls heralding death, and another time when a careless apprentice broke a jar containing a potent potion and hosed the fluid down the drain in hopes his master wouldn't notice. The potion created a self-assembled monster in the sewer, composed of feces, dissolving paper, and live rats, which proved damnably hard to kill, though they managed. Marla was, herself, not especially instrumental in either battle, though she did get to punch a black dog and, the other time, ended up with some sentient crap on her shoes. She didn't mind. Everything was a learning experience, and she'd begun to think about the future. Someday, she was sure, she'd be as important to the city as Artie, and instead of taking orders, she'd be the one giving them.

Jenny started dating various apprentices, though none of the relationships lasted long; her passions were fiery and burned out quickly, and she got a reputation as a heartbreaker. Marla and Daniel and Jenny and her boy-of-the-moment went on double dates in the mundane world and in Artie's London, where the food didn't sustain you but the after-dinner walks were incomparably interesting.

Marla's relationship with Daniel continued, and though the primal passion of their first months faded a bit, they grew ever more comfortable with one another, and if they weren't dependent on each other, they at least knew they could *depend* on each other. The sex stayed interesting. They were both kinky in mostly congruent ways, and were each willing to try almost anything at least once. There were a lot of things to try.

Life during the last of Marla's teenage years was, by and large, very good.

On her twentieth birthday, Daniel took Marla out for lunch at a great greasy taco joint. She was in a pretty good mood, the only irritant a mild burn in her nethers, which she figured for a urinary tract infection. She could get a *curendera* to heal it, but she didn't want to owe the favor or pay the money; she figured she'd just slam some cranberry juice and let it run its course.

After lunch, Daniel took Marla to his favorite used clothing store, and said, "I'll buy you anything you want!"

Marla laughed, looking around at the racks of velvet dresses and vintage tuxedos. "Daniel. I wear, like, the same thing every day. Pants loose enough to roundhouse kick, shirt tight enough it doesn't get caught in heavy machinery, and that's good enough for me."

"Live a little, Marla. Don't you ever want to dress up?"

"I dressed up for *you* just last Saturday night. Though it definitely wasn't my style."

"You look good in lace. Better out of it, but good in it. But, come on, you were just saying the other day how a lot of the sorcerers have such specific style—the Chamberlain in her evening gowns, the Bay Witch in her wetsuit—"

"I think that's just practical," Marla said.

"—Artie in his Aloha shirts, Ernesto with his tuxedo… I figured you could pick something out for yourself. A signature, you know? A badass trenchcoat." He pulled a long black duster down from a hanger.

"Cliché," Marla said.

"Maybe an aviator scarf." He pointed.

"Might as well wear a sign that says 'strangle me.'"

"Okay, then a—"

"Hey," Marla said. "What's this?"

In the back of the store, on a rack marked "Clearance," there was something white, the white of freshly-exposed bone, the white of milk poured out over new snow. She took the cloth from the rack, and it fluttered open, revealing a purple lining. Not bright purple, but darker, bruise-purple, rotten-meat-purple, a crushed-flower color. Marla was never much for colors of any kind—her wardrobe tended to white and black—but something about that purple appealed to her.

"Is it like a cape, or…" Daniel said.

"A cloak," Marla said. "See, it has a hood? Wow." The cloth was almost warm in her hands, incredibly soft, incredibly beautiful, just… incredible. "This," she said. "I want this." The want was physical. Like hunger, the need for air, the need she felt sometimes for Daniel.

"My treat, then. How much is it? Huh, there's no price tag." Daniel called over the clerk, but Marla didn't stop staring at the cloak. The clerk and Daniel haggled, and Marla didn't even hear the number they settled on, didn't snap out of her contemplation of the cloth until Daniel patted her shoulder. "It's all yours, Marla. You'll definitely stand out wearing that thing. All in white, you'll look like the good witch of the very far North."

"Nothing good about me," Marla said, but her heart wasn't in the banter; her mind was on the cloak. They walked out of the shop, Marla still stroking the fabric, and they'd gone a few blocks when Daniel said, "Well, are you going to try it on?"

Marla nodded. She pulled the cloak on over her shoulders, clasping it together at the throat—she didn't have a cloak pin—and felt… strange. She realized, after a moment, that the discomfort from her UTI was simply gone, that it had vanished as soon as she put on the cloak.

"We'll have to get you something to fasten that on," Daniel said. "Looks pretty awesome though. You've got a whole superhero vibe going."

"Yeah," Marla said, thoughtfully, taking off the cloak. Had it… healed her? But how would it do that? Was it enchanted? If so, what was it doing in a used clothing store? Had some sorcerer made it, then died, and his kids inherited it and sold it? Or...

"Some pawn shops with good jewelry down this way," Daniel said. "Let's check it out."

She followed him, still thinking, but looked up when she heard him say "—got the feeling the clerk had never even *seen* the cloak before, seemed totally mystified by it. Just made up a price. I think we got a pretty good deal though. Weird, huh? I mean, it's a pretty memorable-looking item."

"Huh," Marla said. "Yeah. Weird."

Daniel bought her a silver pin in the shape of a stag beetle to fasten the cloak, but Marla didn't put the white-and-purple back on. She wasn't afraid of it, exactly. But she wanted to be cautious.

That night, when she slept—alone, telling Daniel she had a headache, which was true but not the whole truth—she dreamed of wearing the cloak, and nothing else, but instead of the white side, the purple lining was on the outside, and there were shadowy crowds around her, bowing their heads, and whispering her name.

When she woke up, she was wearing the cloak, though she had no memory of getting up in the night to put it on. Somehow, though, it felt right, against her bare skin. She took it off long enough to get dressed, then fastened the cloak back around her throat, bunching the fabric in her fingers. She felt as if a voice were whispering, just beyond the limit of her hearing. She listened harder.

It was not yet dawn.

Marla went out walking, with whispers in her head.

Chapter Eleven

MARLA LISTENED as she walked through the last dregs of the night, moving south and west, toward the city proper. She had no destination in mind, but since the moment she'd run away from home years before she'd associated walking with time alone, time to think, time to make decisions. Engaging her body in movement and motion left her mind free to work over problems.

Or, in this case, to listen to the whispering that filled her head, emanating, it seemed, from somewhere in the vicinity of the base of her skull: as if her brain stem itself were speaking to her.

But Marla knew the half-heard voice belonged to the cloak. Perhaps the garment had once belonged to some other sorcerer, and a bit of that enchanter's personality clung to the fabric, like the scent of nicotine lingering in a dead smoker's drapes. Maybe the words it was whispering were nonsense, or something that would *seem* nonsensical in the absence of context; a voice saying "Rosebud" or "I wish I'd drunk more champagne."

While she listened, she also thought about the cloak's apparent healing prowess, and so she stopped on the side of the road, among the scraggly pine trees by the shoulder, and drew one of her daggers. She pressed it into the palm of her hand, and the blade—she kept it very sharp—drew a line of blood, but the wound closed along the path of her knife. Near-instantaneous healing, but it hadn't done anything about the pain—she'd felt the cool sting of the blade parting flesh.

The whispering grew louder but no more intelligible.

She wiped the bit of blood from her palm off onto the cloak, but it didn't leave a red splotch—the cloak seemed to absorb the blood into itself without leaving a single spot behind, which brought uncomfortable thoughts of vampiric cursed garments, but maybe it was just magically

93

stain-resistant? The cloak seemed to have healing magic, so how could it be dangerous? And just how good *was* it at healing? How did she dare test it? If she jumped off the roof of a building, would the cloak keep her alive on impact? It wasn't something she was comfortable trying out. But she was in a dangerous business, and if the cloak's healing prowess could give her an edge in a fight... well, she couldn't think of any reason she'd ever want to take it off.

If only I could hear what it's saying, she thought.

Marla kept walking, most of her attention turned inward, and soon she reached the Balsamo River that bisected the city. The nearest bridge was a good mile upstream, so she mumbled an incantation to activate the surface-tension enchantments on her boots, the so-called Jesus Spell that would let her walk on the river's surface as easily as the little water-skipper insects she'd sacrificed to make the charm. She considered casting a little look-away spell on herself, but to hell with it—if any ordinary out here in the first inklings of dawn saw a woman clad in a pure white cloak walking on the misty surface of the river, what did it matter? They'd be unlikely to believe their eyes, and if they did, she would certainly sound like an apparition to anyone they told.

She saw no one, and on the other side of the broad slow-moving river she walked up the dirty slope of the riverbank, reached a pair of railroad tracks, and paused there in the middle, wondering: *If a train came, could I survive the impact?*

Another experiment she wasn't willing to try.

The whisper was clearer, though, so she kept going. She walked through the trainyard, slipping through a chained gate, and walked on into the kind of business district that springs up around freight yards: lots of windowless buildings with corrugated steel walls, empty lots surrounded by chain link fences, mountains of shipping containers. If she went east a little distance she'd reach the docks and cranes of the port.

Instead she kept going south, passing soul-food restaurants, aquarium supply stores, boarded-up gas stations with the pumps ripped out, and alleys, alleys, alleys. She could almost make out what the cloak was saying, could nearly hear the word, and she thought it was indeed a single word: Urn? Burn? Spurn?

She stopped in an alley, and closed her eyes, and sat down there on the stained concrete, and drove all thought from her mind. Here, in the heart (or if not the heart than at least the liver or kidney) of the city she loved, totally at home, totally comfortable, she could simply open her mind and let whatever the cloak was broadcasting flow in. She could empty herself, and make a silence, and in that silence, she could hear the word.

When it came again, the word was so clear that she spoke it aloud as it sounded in her head:

"Turn."

And the cloak turned.

First came hyper-awareness. Marla looked around, and the world was subtly changed; except it wasn't the world, but her perception. She could see the weak points in the walls, the stresses in the steel of the dumpsters, the points of maximum breakage. Where to hit things, to make them shatter. Useful knowledge.

Next came the strength. Power coursed through her. She'd been the recipient of spells to enhance the reflexes before, to alter subjective time sense, to increase reaction time, but they all paled compared to this. She could do anything. She could leap from the ground, to the top of that dumpster, and from there to the hanging metal of that fire escape, and from there propel herself to the roof—

And she did, and she did, and she did.

She crouched on the edge of the roof of a three-story building and saw her own hands and arms had been transformed. Her body was still there, but it seemed faint, a skeleton clothed in translucent new flesh: she was wreathed in a bruise-purple suit of shadow, and when she extended her hand, the shadows extended into claws. She knew without questioning the source of the knowledge that those claws could tear open a bank vault, that she could climb overhand up the side of a skyscraper, that she could punch someone through the ribcage and have her fist emerge from their back, clutching their crushed spine in her first.

The cloak had changed, too, from white to purple, the lining somehow switching places with the exterior, and now the healing white was hidden away on the inside, and Marla was clothed in purple.

The color of bruises, rotten meat, dead flowers; the color of emperors.

None of this surprised her. She felt cool, and utterly in control, and above all observant: looking at the world, and discovering how its pieces fit together, and how to break them, and how to remake them to her own liking.

She ran across the rooftops, leaping from one to another as the first rays of light touched the sky, and she did not stop running and calculating vectors for damage until she saw the boy in the alleyway below.

That's no boy, she thought, and the words did not seem entirely her own. But if her own thoughts were spoken in harmony with the voice of the cloak, what of it? The cloak was older than her—older by far—and surely wiser, and she should heed its counsel. After all, with the cloak, she would own the world, and all would fall before her, and her will would become indistinguishable from the inalterable laws of nature.

The boy was small, perhaps eight years old, but more likely a malnourished ten. He wore a ragged dirty too-big t-shirt doubtless scrounged from some shelter bin, and torn denim shorts, and no shoes. He had dark hair, dark eyes, and brown skin, and he pawed disconsolately through the spillover from the garbage cans behind a restaurant. He tried to eat a paper wrapper, ignoring the bits of sandwich wrapped inside.

He was not a boy. Something about him was wrong, alien, disjointed: the body was human, but what dwelled in it was not.

This thing could be useful to us, Marla thought, or the cloak thought, or they both thought. She dropped from the roof and landed before the boy, who stumbled back against the wall, eyes wide, mouth open.

"What are you?" she asked, and her voice was like the sizzle of flesh burning, the hiss of escaping nerve gas, the growl of a beast.

"I—I don't know," the boy said. "I just… found this. This body. I'm just… here." And then, in a voice of real anguish: "I'm *hungry*."

Take his jaw, Marla—the cloak—*they* thought, and they reached out, almost gently, as if to caress the boy's face, but instead their hands closed around his lower jaw, and twisted, and pulled the jawbone away as easily as plucking a leaf from the branch of a tree.

The boy screamed and fell and bled, but Marla paid no mind, squinting at the jaw, and then, with precise talons of shadow, stripping away the skin and blood—the cloak soaked in the blood—and holding the dirty white tiny jaw aloft. *This will make a useful oracle*, they thought, and already knew how to enchant it the bone to allow it to speak. The jaw would be able to tell them whatever its mysterious supernatural original owner knew, as soon as he knew it. This boy, and whatever strange spirit possessed him, would be their unwilling informant forever. They put the jaw away in one of the cloak's pockets, though it didn't actually *have* pockets, usually.

It's no good if the boy dies, they thought, and Marla knelt, reaching out to touch him—but stopped. Their touch was good for killing, for death, but not for gentler things, not for salvation.

The part of Marla that was still just Marla thought, *The white side of the cloak, it could heal him*, and the rest of her thought, *No!*

But it was too late. Marla thought, "Turn."

And the cloak turned, deadly purple replaced by soothing white, and Marla saw what she'd done to the boy, and she began to wail.

"I found this boy," Marla said, cradling him in her arms, standing in the hallway in front of Hamil's apartment door. He was the sorcerer who lived nearest to the place where she'd encountered the boy, and he had always struck her as a basically kind man, and now he nodded slowly, and ushered her in.

"I know you, ah, hire street kids to be your eyes and ears," she said. "So when I found him, hurt, I thought, maybe you could…" She trailed off. *Save him*, she thought. *Save me.*

"What happened to him?" Hamil said.

She shook her head. What could she say? "I put on a magical cloak. It hijacked my brain. I ripped this kid's jaw off, and now I don't know where the jaw *went*?" No. So she said, "I used some healing magic to stop the bleeding, keep him alive, but… fuck, Hamil, his *jaw* is gone."

Hamil nodded again. "So I see."

Marla hadn't used any healing spells. She'd draped the white cloak across the boy's body, hoping it would heal him, hoping it *wouldn't* transform him into… whatever she'd been turned into. The cloak's work had begun immediately, with the boy's bloody mess of a wound closing up, blood absorbed into the cloak, and the boy's glassy-eyed shocked stare had vanished as he closed his eyes and fell into deep sleep, breathing slow regular breaths. She'd half-hoped the cloak would heal him sufficiently to make his stolen jaw grow back, but that was either beyond the cloak's capabilities or—and she felt stupid thinking this, though at the same time she thought it was entirely possible—or else the cloak didn't *want* to grow the boy's jaw back, out of pique, or vindictiveness, or simple expedience. How could she put anything past this garment?

She couldn't believe it had been so easy. That all it had taken to transform the cloak was a single word, and a simple word, at that: "Turn." How could it be that easy to change from a healer to a force of merciless analytical destruction? It was like having a big red button marked "Fire" in a missile silo, so one push would launch all the warheads at once, no double-checking, no failsafes. Who would make a magical device so dangerous and yet so simple to activate?

Nobody would. The cloak wasn't an enchanted piece of cloth, and had likely never been sewn and dyed by human hands. The cloak was an artifact. It was an object with a point-of-view. An object with an *agenda*.

I'll be more careful next time, Marla had thought, and wrapped up the cloak into a bundle tucked under her arm, and then she'd carried the boy to Hamil's building, using a look-away spell to keep herself unnoticed in the streets and through the lobby and up the elevator.

"What would you like me to do with him?" Hamil said, gesturing to his clean white couch, where Marla put the boy down. "Why not take him to an emergency room?"

"An emergency room can't give him a new jaw," Marla said.

"Ah. I do know a magical surgeon who can take a cadaver's jaw, grow new skin over the bone, and implant it on the boy. It will be as if he'd never lost anything. But such procedures are expensive, Marla."

"I can pay," she said. Marla made money, but she almost never spent any. Her favorite thing was work, and her only hobby was sleeping with Daniel, which, given Artie's inventory, was free no matter how elaborate they got.

Hamil shrugged. "Of course. It's your money. Shall I let you know how he recovers? He should be fine, but there are always risks."

"Sure," Marla said, trying to affect nonchalance, but was it dangerous to let a doctor operate on the kid without giving him all the information he might need? "Ah, I should mention, I... don't think he's human. Entirely."

"Oh?" Hamil looked much more interested now. "Why do you say that?"

"Just, ah... a feeling. I don't know what he is, but..."

"Let's see," Hamil said, and left the room.

Marla shifted her weight from foot to foot, holding the cloak as unobtrusively as possible under her arm, unsure whether she should stay. She looked at the poor mutilated sleeping boy, and hoped he would keep sleeping for a long time, until he was whole again. How had she *done* such a thing?

She hadn't. The cloak had used her. She'd be more careful next time. Next time, *she'd* be the one doing the using.

Hamil returned, carrying a pair of eyeglasses with multiple lenses on movable arms. "Modified jeweler's lenses," he said. "They allow me to see evidence of possession, illusion, things like that. Let's see..." He knelt by the boy—lowering his great bulk was quite the production—and adjusted the lenses. He grunted. "Definitely something here. Non-human, but not a ghostly possession like I've ever seen... and it's rare for me to see something totally new. This bears further study." He glanced at Marla. "I'll see he's taken care of. Give Artie my best, would you?"

Marla nodded, and left the boy behind, but took the shame with her.

On the street outside Hamil's apartment, a vagrant in a filthy flannel shirt stumbled toward her. Marla smelled ozone and heard the crackled of static electricity and said "Oh, shit."

The Throne staggered into her path, coughed, and said, "We know what you did. We are watching you. We saw. You will be judged. You will face retribution."

"Fuck off and die," Marla said. "I feel bad enough."

The Throne stared at her for a moment, light leaking from the corners of his eyes, and then shrugged as if to say, *I tried*, and walked in a drunkard's weave around her and away.

Back home, she avoided everyone, slipping up to her room unbothered. She shook out the cloak, and the jawbone fell out of the folds as if she'd just tucked it there, as if she hadn't turned the cloak upside down and shaken it earlier trying to find the bone. Maybe she should give the jaw to Hamil, for the boy... but then he'd want to know how she got it, and anyway, it was just bone and teeth now, no better than the jawbone of some corpse a psychic surgeon could procure. She put it on a shelf in her closet. *Might as well enchant it,* she thought, and though she felt another stab of guilt, she knew herself well enough to know she'd follow through on making the jawbone into an oracle. The terrible act had been committed, and couldn't be taken back, and she'd made amends as best she could; she may as well get some use from it. The boy was supernatural, perhaps in an unprecedented way, and there was no telling what she might be able to learn from him.

Marla put the cloak in her closet on a hanger, where it hung looking entirely harmless. She couldn't bear being in the same room with it. Not now.

She went down to the basement and worked out, and shooed Daniel away when he checked on her, and didn't go up to dinner, and fell asleep at about eight p.m., entirely exhausted, and dreamed of a bruise-colored thing crouching in her closet, whispering to her; which was really, she thought, just a bit too on-the-nose.

"Marla!" Jenny called, and she swam up into consciousness. "Huh?"

"Phone," Jenny said from the doorway, and tossed the cordless across to her.

Even half-asleep Marla's reflexes were good, so she caught the phone out of the air, put it to her ear, and said, "Yeah?"

"It's Hamil. I thought you'd like to know the boy—or whatever he is—is fine. His new jaw works well, and he's lucid, talking, and eating all the food I put in front of him. I gather he's been living on the street for a while… and, further, that he wasn't entirely sure what objects around him were edible, or even exactly how to eat. He claims not to know his true nature or origins, and while it may be an elaborate subterfuge on the part of some extra-dimensional monster, I tend to believe him. He seems essentially childlike. He's agreed to let me study him and run some tests, in exchange for food and a place to sleep. I won't charge you for the surgery, by the way. He's a fascinating subject, and has quite the sense of humor for someone who was, almost literally, born yesterday. I'm glad to have him."

"That's good," Marla said. "Thanks. Does he, ah, remember what happened to him?" Hoping, not. Hoping the cloak could heal bad memories too.

"Not very clearly. He says he was attacked by a horrible shadowy monster, and then he says a pretty lady—that's you—came and helped him."

"Ah," Marla said. "That's… Ah."

"Mmm," Hamil said. "Tell me, Marla—should I organize a force to scour the city for this alleged monster?"

Her throat went dry. Hamil was at least as badass as Artie, possibly more so, and thus not a guy to be fucked with. "I don't think that'll be necessary."

"I wondered," Hamil said. "Care to tell me what happened?"

"You know I do battle magics," she said, telling a lie that happened to be true, just irrelevant. "Things got out of hand. I lost control."

"I thought it might be something like that. Thank you for telling me the truth. You might want to talk to Artie about it. He could give you some advice, I think, and as your mentor, it's his duty."

"I'll do that," Marla said, miserable, but knowing he was right. Worse, she'd have to tell Artie the *real* truth about the cloak. It was too big a secret to try to hide.

"See that you do," Hamil said. "Oh, by the way, the boy's name—he says we should call him Rondeau."

"Ron Doe? What, like John Doe's brother?"

"No," Hamil said, and spelled it. "It's a kind of poem, a form, like a sonnet or a villanelle. He says he heard someone say it—I can't imagine where, perhaps near the University—and thought it would make a good name. Isn't that, I don't know, cute?"

"Yeah," Marla said. "Tell Rondeau the pretty lady is glad to hear he's okay."

"I'll do more than that. I'll tell him the pretty lady who saved him was also the terrible creature who maimed him."

Marla sucked in a hard breath. "What—why would you do that?"

"Because you did a monstrous thing," Hamil said, voice terrible and mild. "And he should not feel grateful to you. Don't you agree?"

"When you put it that way," Marla said, and Hamil hung up the phone.

Chapter Twelve

"THAT'S AN ARTIFACT ALL RIGHT," Artie said, gazing down at the cloak, which was spread out on Marla's bed and looked as ordinary as a white-and-purple cloak could.

"You don't need to, I dunno, make a special artifact-identifying tincture and put a drop in each eye and see its magic revealed?" Marla said.

Artie shrugged. He was about two feet from the foot of the bed. He didn't seem inclined to go any closer. "I could. But I've been doing this a long time, and you develop a certain sense. A thousand tiny little details, all adding up, I couldn't even tell you what all of the things I'm noticing *are*, but my brain notes them all. Like, for instance, what's it feel like?"

"Sorta silky… woolly… cottony… I dunno. It changes."

"But look, you can't see any weave, any stitching, it's of a piece, like it's a sheet of leather or plastic or something. There's no seam where the hood's sewn on. It's like it just *grew* that way." He shook his head. "And you actually wore it?"

"How was I supposed to know? I just thought it was a cool cloak. I don't have all those years of experience. I didn't get any kind of eldritch vibe." Or had she? The cloak had certainly seemed to call to her, to demand her attention, and since she normally thought of clothing only as a boring necessity, that was noteworthy. "At least, nothing that made me afraid to put it on," she amended.

"And it healed your, ah…" He gestured vaguely crotchward.

"Yeah. I thought then maybe it was enchanted, something out of a sorcerer's estate, wound up in a thrift store, you know?"

"Sure. Until you figured out the mental command to make it switch colors, and then…"

"Then I went crazy, and attacked a kid, and who knows what I would have done if I hadn't made it switch from purple to white again."

Artie stared at the cloak for a while, then said, abruptly, "Okay, here's what we do. We pick this thing up with some tongs or something, put it in a special suitcase I've got—it doesn't nullify magic, but it sorta shields it—and then we'll take it down to Viscarro, find out if he's ever heard of anything like this, and either way, we'll get him to tuck it away into a little vault until—"

"No," Marla said, surprising even herself. "Artie, it's *mine*."

He looked at her levelly. "That's true. But it doesn't have to be. I don't care how powerful it is, Viscarro can contain it. He doesn't do anything but think about hoarding artifacts. I'm not saying we give it to him, sell it to him, anything like that, just hire him to hold it for us until we can figure it out—"

"You've got an artifact, so why can't I have one?"

Artie shook his head. "Does that cloak still have its hooks in your brain? I've got *half* an artifact, and sure, it's powerful. It'll change your sex, or your gender, or both if you make the mistake of sticking it in one of your orifices, and it's done weirder stuff too—but your cloak talks to you and tries to make you into a killing machine. You see the difference?"

"Sure," Marla said. "But it was better the second time."

Artie stared at her. "You put it on *again*?"

"After Hamil tore me a new one on the phone. I cast a time-release sleeping spell on myself just in case, and then I went down to the beach, away from any people, and put on the cloak, and told it to turn. I got that clarity again, and the power, and sure, I got to thinking of everybody in the world as nothing but a disposable game piece on a board, but I knew what was coming this time, I kept myself in control. I think I built up a kind of resistance, after wearing it once. I didn't have any trouble changing the cloak back to white, and I was back upstairs in my own bed before the sleeping spell hit me. It's safe, Artie."

"At least it wants you to think it is," Artie said. "You shouldn't underestimate something like this. There's no telling where it came from, what it wants..." He sighed. "But I'm sure there's a reason you're the one who found it."

"What, like I've got a special destiny?" Marla said.

Artie smacked her on the back of the head, lightly. "No. Destiny. Shit. We've been over that. There's no destiny, just likelihoods, just narrowing of possibilities down into certainties. No, I don't mean fate. But things like this, artifacts, they're objects with a *point of view*. They're things with *intentions*. No, you don't have a destiny. But *this*. This has plans for you. Maybe they'll be good for you. Maybe they won't."

"It's a tool," Marla said. "It's something I can use. I don't have what Daniel has, what Jenny has, that inborn power, I can't reach out and manipulate the world like they can, it's *hard* for me. This could make things so much easier. I could go far."

"You can use it," Artie said. "Just never forget for a minute that it's also using you." He turned to face her and put both hands on his shoulders. When he spoke, his voice was gentle. "If you're going to wear that thing, Marla, I need you to move out of my house."

She was surprised at the jolt of dismay that went through her gut. Over the past years, Artie's house in the cliff had become her home, the only home she'd ever cared about. "What? You're throwing me out? Why?"

"Because that thing's older than me, and probably knows more than I do, and I can't be your master if you're learning from it too." He patted her on the shoulder. "Don't think I'm throwing you out. It's more like I'm pushing you out of the nest. I'm not disowning you or anything. After what happened with Ernesto… That was bad. He and I both behaved badly. I don't want that kind of bad blood between you and me. You're welcome here, you can visit anytime, and we'll keep all our oaths and promises to one another. I'll steer work your way, I'll vouch for you, all that. But you won't be my apprentice anymore. You'll be freelance. A consultant." He smiled faintly. "What Sauvage calls a 'wand for hire.'" He glanced at the bed. "Just, when you come over, leave that thing locked up at home, would you? And get a good magically-protected wardrobe or something to keep it in, you don't want it falling into the wrong hands."

"What if I don't want to go?" Marla said.

He shrugged. "I call up Viscarro, and he studies the cloak, tries to figure out what it is, probably ends up locking it in a lead box below the surface of the Earth for as close to forever as we can manage. Most sorcerers are cautious about stuff like this, Marla. For good reason. But it's your choice."

Marla picked up the cloak in her hands, the smooth substantial fabric warm in her hands, the white so impossibly pure, the purple as dark as blood pooling in a bruised cadaver. "Locking it away… Artie, that would be such a waste."

"That's it, then," Artie said. "You want me to tell Daniel, or will you?"

"I bought you an *artifact*?" Daniel said, helping to carry Marla's bags to the Bentley. "That's kinda like loaning a guy a buck so he can buy a lottery ticket, and then he wins the jackpot."

Marla slung a bag into the backseat. "What are you saying? You paid for it, so it should be yours?"

He held up his hands. "Whoa, hon, not at all. Don't want it, wouldn't take it if you offered it. I can make birds fall out of the sky by looking at them. I can live indefinitely off the life energy in a field of grass. I'm good." He went to the passenger seat—his driving privileges had been restored, but Marla driving them was habit, though she still didn't like it much. She climbed behind the wheel, and he went on. "Besides, I wouldn't trust myself with something like that. Something magical you have to wrestle with, a test of wills every time you use it? I don't know that I'm up for it. But you? I don't worry about you."

Marla tried to hide her smile. "Well, of course. Why would you worry about me?" She started the car and began the drive south to her new place.

"So what are you going to do?"

"Artie's putting out the word that I'm available for freelance work. Legbreaking and bodyguarding and general menacing and stuff like that mostly, at first anyway. Courier work. Nothing too glamorous."

"Weird that he's making you leave. Seems like with the cloak you'd be an even bigger asset."

"To be totally honest, I think the cloak kinda freaks him out." She reached over and patted the folded fabric, where it rested on the seat between Daniel and herself. "He wouldn't even touch it. He did say he might have work for me soon though. And let me tell you, Danny boy, freelance rates are way better than what he's been paying us."

"But I get room and board in the cheesy porn castle, and you have to pay your own rent."

"Ha. Artie hooked me up there, too. We looked at some places yesterday, and one of them, I just fell in love with. Artie knew the owner, and he sold me a whole apartment *building*, and it only cost me damn near every penny I've saved."

"You bought a building? Why? You planning on renting out the other apartments?"

"Nah, it's an old flophouse, been closed down for years, but there are a couple of apartments in good repair where I can stay. It hasn't found a buyer before because it's a little bit haunted. Lots of old folks died in there, left some nasty psychic residue, but that's mostly on the lower floors. But Daniel: it's got *gargoyles*. Somebody actually stuck gargoyles on the place! It's awesome. And I like the idea of having all that privacy. Believe me after, growing up in a trailer park where your back yard is somebody else's front yard, this place is a dream come true. " She glanced at him. "And we can make just as much noise as we want."

"And we don't have to worry about Artie pressing his ear to the wall next door, listening and wishing he could jerk off," Daniel said. "That does have a certain appeal."

"It's a shithole," Daniel said several hours later, sitting up on the futon in the living room of her fifth-floor apartment. "But I could get used to playing house here with you."

"Who says we're playing?" Marla planted a kiss on his lips. She pulled the covers off him. "Now get in the kitchen and make me some eggs. And put on that little apron I bought for you while you do it. Hey, stop that! Did I say anything about putting your pants on first?"

Daniel stayed over three of the next five nights, but otherwise, Marla had the place to herself. She worked some magics to keep the roof from leaking, and cast some protective wards to keep the place from burning down or being burglarized, and then went antique shopping with Jenny Click. Together they picked out a lovely old wooden wardrobe, carved all over with vines and flowers, and had it delivered to Marla's new apartment. They spent a long afternoon hacking various protective runes into its wood and imbuing them with power. If anybody other than Marla tried to open the wardrobe they'd burst into flame, and that would be the *least* of their problems.

They were sitting on the futon, enjoying the view of dirty rooftops from the window across the way and drinking dirty martinis, when Jenny said, "Oh, Artie wants you to come to a meeting tomorrow night."

"This that business he was talking about?"

"Yeah." Jenny sighed. "It's Rasmussen again."

Marla put down her drink on the old wooden orange crate she was using as an end table. "Oh you're fucking kidding me."

"Nope. You ever meet his apprentice, Pritchard?"

"Weasel face, red hair?"

"That's the one. He's switched sides. Says Rasmussen has totally gone off the deep end. I don't know the details, but apparently Pritchard's terrified, and came to Artie for help."

"So… what? I didn't hire on to be an assassin. And I know Daniel can theoretically snuff out life, but I don't think he'd go for it, either."

"I doubt the three of us together could take down Rasmussen, even with Artie's help," Jenny said. "I don't know what he has us to do. If I had to guess—da dum!—I'd say we're going to be sent to steal Rasmussen's half of the artifact."

"So what you're gonna do," Artie said, "is you're gonna go and steal Rasmussen's half of the artifact." He inclined his head toward Pritchard, who sat twitching on the far side of the table in the conference room in Juliana's club. "We got our inside man to supply us with keys and codes and spell-picks. The artifact's in Rasmussen's office. The asshole himself is on site, too, but Pritchard's going to distract him and get him out of the house for a while. In exchange for a lot of dough, and my help setting him up with a new life underground, once this little job is done."

"When's this happen?" Daniel asked.

"Tomorrow," Artie said. "You leave for England tonight." He glanced at Marla. "The terms acceptable to you, freelancer?"

"If you've got the money, honey, I've got the knife."

"Good. Pritchard will give you the details on the plane. I chartered you guys a jet." He paused. "And Marla. Be sure to bring your cloak. I hate that thing, but it could come in handy."

"This is too easy," Daniel said, subverting the locks on one of the numerous back doors at Rasmussen's estate.

Marla stifled a yawn. She'd slept on the plane, but not enough, and the jet lag was playing hell with her—

Wait. She suddenly felt better, rested and re-oriented and tip-top. She took a fold of the cloak's white cloth in her fingers and considered it. Had the cloak sensed her complaint, and… healed her jet lag? It was a bit disturbing to think the cloak could read her mind, though in retrospect it wasn't surprising—she'd experimented, and she could reverse it to purple if she just *thought* the word "turn" with the proper intent.

"There," Daniel said as the dark wooden door popped open and swung inward. "With the hair and flesh samples Pritchard gave me, I was able to make my life force mimic Rasmussen's. The house thinks I'm him now, and you're my guests, so we should be good."

"Too bad," Jenny said, holding up her hand where a little wreath of flame sparkled. "I was hoping for plan B." Plan B was burning the whole place down and finding the other half of Artie's artifact in the ashes. The artifact wouldn't burn.

They slipped through the door, which led into a mud room. "We should have the place to ourselves," Daniel whispered, "but be on alert anyway. You have the map, Marla?"

"Memorized it," she said. "Let me lead." She took point, consulting the blueprints in her mind. If they were here, then the office where the artifact was located would be...

They moved through the dark house, all murmuring spells to amplify their night vision so their eyes could suck up every particle of stray light. The effect was a bit greenish and gritty, but they wouldn't trip over any antique ottomans or topple any decorative suits of armor. Rasmussen's estate was pure old English country, with heavy dark wood furnishings, swords and axes and tapestries and animal heads on the walls, and lots of elaborately framed portraits and paintings of hunting scenes—though the one painting Marla looked at closely had huntsmen and hounds pursuing not a fox but a naked woman. She shivered. Rasmussen was a weird bad dude.

They went up the broad uncreaking stairs, down a hall, and there at the end was the entry to Rasmussen's study. She reached out her hand for the knob—

"Wait," Daniel hissed. "Somebody's in there, trying to conceal their life-force, but I got the edge of it. Shit. We're blown. We should—"

"Come in," said Rasmussen from inside the office, and the door swung open of its own accord.

"Might as well now," Jenny said. "At least have some news to take back to Artie. If we make it back."

Marla and Daniel shared a glance, then both nodded. They stepped into the room.

Rasmussen wore a black robe and far too much silver jewelry, and sat behind his broad desk before an oversized mortar and pestle, grinding something, making the occasional grunt of effort. "Ah, yes, Artie's three stooges. How nice to see you all. Sent you to snatch my artifact, did he?"

"Just a routine surveillance mission," Marla said with a shrug.

"Hmm. Not what Pritchard told me. After I flayed him earlier today."

Marla did her best to show no reaction. "Torture's a lousy way to get information out of somebody. They'll say anything to make the pain stop."

Rasmussen smiled, faintly. "I didn't torture him to get him to talk. I tortured him as punishment for betraying me. After he was dead I had a necromancer interrogate his skull to find out the precise nature of his betrayal. I knew he disapproved of my current occult pursuits, but to go to Artie, that clown... Most disappointing."

"Why don't you give us your half?" Daniel said. "You said it yourself, you don't care about Artie anymore, you aren't trying to complete the artifact, so why not let him have it?"

"First, because immortality would be wasted on him. Second, because the artifact is no more." He tipped up the mortar to show them what rested inside.... and there it was. Part of it, anyway. A semi-circle of reddish-black stone, marked much like Artie's stone phallus. Once it had been a whole circle, but Rasmussen was halfway done crushing it to powder.

"Bullshit," Daniel said. "It's a fake. You can't smash up an artifact like you're crushing a bunch of pills!"

"You can when it's another artifact doing the crushing," Rasmussen said. "This was Baba Yaga's mortar and pestle. It can crush *anything*. I needed to reduce the artifact to a more... ingestible form... to aid me some other matters I'm pursuing. Crushed like this, it's reduced to pure powdered power." He picked up a silver letter opener, scooped up a portion of the artifact dust on the blade, lifted it to his nose, and snorted. His eyes flashed red, and when he smiled, coils of smoke emerged from between his teeth. "Oh, that's good," he said. "That's very, very good. You have no idea the things I can see now, the languages I can read, the incantatory phrases I can pronounce..." He frowned. "Now scurry back and tell Artie to piss off. I have nothing he wants anymore. We're shut of each other forever. I should kill one of you just for the sake of good form, but then he'd switch his obsession from immortality to revenge, and this has all grown too tedious already. Now *go*."

"We're not going anywhere," Marla said, but Rasmussen merely snorted, and spoke a few slippery words, and everything went black before Marla could even think about thinking the word "turn."

Chapter Thirteen

"**So we woke up** in the hold of a cargo ship hauling aircraft engines from Britain to Felport, and we were stuck on the ship for the past week," Marla said. "Dunno if Rasmussen magicked us there or just had some goons dump us." She took an enormous bite of her rare roast beef sandwich. They'd stayed hidden on the ship using simple look-away spells, but they'd had to subsist on what they could steal—except Daniel, who'd lived off the life energy of passing dolphins or something—and real food was something she'd missed.

"But you're sure his half of the artifact is gone?" Artie sat on the other side of the table, looking off into the waters of the bay. Marla loved eating out on the deck and watching the ocean, even on cool days like this, but now she sat with her back to the waves. She'd seen enough of the big blue sea in the past few days.

"Yeah," Daniel said. "Crushed to dust and snorted. How fucked-up is that?"

Artie shook his head. "It's crazy, halfway suicidal—artifacts are worse than carcinogenic, they're thaumagenic, you can grow tumors that *think*— but it will give him power. He must need it for the ritual he has planned."

"What ritual?" Jenny said, and coughed into her fist. She'd picked up a nasty chest cold on the sea crossing, and they'd come straight here to debrief Artie, so she hadn't been to a *bruja* for healing yet. Marla had offered the use of her cloak, but Jenny said it creeped her out, and didn't want it touching her flesh.

"Pritchard didn't just tell me Rasmussen's household schedule— though *that* intel wasn't any good, I guess. But he also told me about Rasmussen's new obsession." Artie stood up and went to the railing. "He wants to raise an old god from beneath the waves."

"What, like H.P. Lovecraft?" Marla said. "Motherfucking Cthulhu and shit?"

Artie shrugged. "The right general idea. There are stories about something sleeping, hibernating, dormant, whatever. Something that used to enslave humans to do its bidding, something that built that megalithic city—you remember the book we sold to Rasmussen? The one about the structures in Micronesia? That's where he's going, to try to call up... something."

"I didn't know we believed in gods," Daniel said, frowning.

Artie turned away from the water—maybe he didn't like the look of it either—and leaned back against the deck railing. "We don't. But this thing is so different from us, so much more powerful, we might as well call it a god. Maybe it's from outer space. Maybe it's from the universe next door and it slithered here through a crack in reality. Maybe it's an artificial life form created by an ancient Earthly super-scientific culture that had summer homes on Atlantis. Who knows? There are mysteries even sorcerers can't penetrate."

Marla thought about her cloak.

"Though just knowing the mysteries *exist* puts us a step ahead," Artie said. "I haven't done the research, but Pritchard says Rasmussen *has*, and that there definitely is something down deep in a crack at the bottom of the sea, snuggled up in a volcanic vent. Something powerful. Something Rasmussen thinks will reward him if he wakes it up."

"Reward him how?" Jenny said.

"Earthly dominion. Eternal life. Nubile young fuck-slaves. The usual. It probably won't work. Stuff like this almost never does. Best case, usually, is you get a tentacle through the heart." Artie grinned. "But you know what, kids? We're going to step in anyway. Rasmussen's going to fail, but *we're* going to be the reason why. We're going to fuck him up. And do you know why?"

"Why?" Marla said, though she thought she knew.

"For spite," Artie said. "Because he ate the other half of my artifact, and I'm pissed. So who's up for a trip to the tropics?"

"Count me out," Marla said.

"I'll double your rate," Artie said.

"Nope," she said.

"Why not?"

"Because I'm sick of the ocean, Artie. I want to stick to dry land for a while." That was true, but it wasn't the whole truth. She'd hoped the loss of the other half of the artifact would *stop* Artie's obsession with Rasmussen, but that didn't seem likely. And he hadn't even apologized for getting them stuck in a cargo ship, and that had *sucked*.

Artie sighed. "Fair enough. Daniel and Jenny can handle it. Rituals like this are delicate. Shouldn't be tough at all for you guys to ruin his plans."

"You're the boss," Daniel said, though he looked at Marla as if—she thought—he were more than a little bit jealous of her freedom.

"We leave tomorrow morning." Daniel nuzzled Marla's neck as a distraction move from stealing the covers.

She stole them back. "Off on Artie's fool's errand?"

"I prefer to think of it as saving the world from a slimy tentacled octopocalypse."

"Whatever gets you through the night, lover boy."

They lay together on Marla's futon and looked up at the waterstained ceiling, and she said, "Going to be gone long?"

He sighed. "Artie says it could be weeks. Jenny and I are going down early to do surveillance and hang around, you know. Rasmussen's waiting for some astronomical alignment, but apparently it's a little unclear when exactly the stars will be right."

"So you're telling me I said no to a tropical vacation of indefinite length? Balls."

"Wouldn't have been much time for fun. But when I get back…"

"We'll have lots of fun," she agreed. Marla reached over and touched his cheek. "I wish you could stay here with me. Every night. And be here every morning."

He rolled over and looked into her eyes. Those long lashes of his still just killed her, and his smile now was a little sly and a little sweet. "That could be arranged. I could be here with you, if you really wanted me to."

"You mean… you'd leave Artie?"

"Not like that. But, you know. Ernesto moved out and got his own place. I feel like maybe it's time for me to do the same. I figured I could get a room over one of the Chinese restaurants downtown—"

"No," Marla said, and kissed him. "No, don't be ridiculous. Stay with me."

"People might find out we're dating if I do that."

"'Dating.' Like you've taken me on a date, ever. Anyway, the whole keeping-things-secret deal was Artie's idea, not mine. I'm not saying we spread our business around, but if people hear we're living together, let them draw whatever conclusions they want."

"Okay," Daniel said. "I'll talk to Artie about it when we finish this thing with Rasmussen."

"Or you *could* tell him before that, and just not go."

"I have to. It's important to Artie. I owe him. I owe him a *lot.*"

Marla propped herself up on one elbow and looked at him thoughtfully. "I owe him, too. He got me off the street and changed my life. But you owe him more than that, don't you?"

"I do."

"You've never told me how you and Artie met."

"You never asked."

"So I'm asking," she said.

"Okay." Daniel closed his eyes. "I grew up poor. Picking salad greens out of the ditch by the roadside poor. Lived way in the middle of nowhere down south."

"I thought you had a little accent, sometimes, when you're mad or drunk."

"I left when I was a kid, but I guess the early stuff sticks with you no matter what," he said. "Anyway, I had a lot of brothers and sisters, lots of cousins, daddy who never had any particular job, mom who did whatever she could, which wasn't much. We lived in a trailer that wasn't ever going to move anywhere again, with rooms added onto the original trailer with plywood and sheet metal, so the house was like an oven in the summer and an icebox in winter. What happened was, I got sick. Really sick. Pneumonia. I was, I don't know. I remember going to kindergarten, and this was after that, so maybe I was about six. They thought I was going to die. But then... I started to get better. Only my older sister, who was mostly making sure I got fed and watered, she started to get sick." His eyes were still closed, but his voice began to break. "It was like something out of a Gothic novel. She just got paler and paler, thinner and thinner, like she wasn't there, and me, I got healthier, stronger, before long I was running and whooping and my sister just sat propped up in a chair in the shadows, watching.

"My daddy always had wild ideas. He was the kind of guy who'd listen to radio shows about alien abductions or government mind control rays and nod seriously, you know? So he decided I was... he never said vampire, but that's what he meant. He decided I was stealing my sister's life to make myself better, making her sick to make me healthy."

Marla couldn't help herself: "Were you?"

"Almost certainly. I'm sure I was feeding on her life energy. It's easier to take life from people, from one person, than it is to be careful and take just a little bit from everything around me in nature, tiny quantities that don't do any lasting harm. I had to learn that. The other way came more naturally." He opened his eyes, but didn't look at her. "Just because daddy was crazy doesn't mean he was wrong."

"So what did your father do?"

"He tried to kill me," Daniel said. "Hit me over the head with a shovel, stuffed me in a sack, and drove me to the town dump. I'm lucky he didn't decapitate me and stuff my mouth with garlic. I woke up surrounded by the bodies of dead scavenger birds and rats. I must have sucked the life out of them to heal myself. And when I came stumbling down from the trash heap, there was Artie, leaning against a battered pick-up truck, and he took my hand—like a parent taking a little kid's hand to help him across the street, you know?—and led me to the passenger side, and told me everything was going to be okay." Daniel shrugged. "I've been with him ever since. He raised me."

"How did he come across you in the first place?"

"Artie told me a psychic said he should be on the lookout for a 'rose in a trash heap,' and he had some locative divination done, and when he showed up at the coordinates, there I was. Artie sometimes called me 'Rosie,' until I was about nine—then I got pissed and told him to stop because it sounded like a girl's name. Sometimes I regret that."

"I had no idea you'd been with him so long."

"He was good about not giving me special treatment." Daniel smiled wryly. "I was off at boarding school a lot of the time, though for summers, I did… magic school. And when I was fifteen I told him I'd learned all I ever wanted to in a classroom, and I wanted to be an apprentice, and he said, 'Okay.' You see why I can't bail on him? This Rasmussen thing, it's important to him, and he's important to me."

"I understand," Marla said. "And I like Artie a lot better right now than I have for a long time."

"He's not perfect, but he's family," Daniel said. He kissed her cheek. "As soon as I get back from the crazy cultist command performance of *South Pacific*, I'll come here first, okay?"

"You'd better."

"Go ahead and clean out a couple of drawers in the dresser for me," Daniel said.

About five weeks later Marla came home and saw the runes hacked around her doorway glowing a soft green. She was wearing her cloak, tired from a day guarding a courier van that drove all over hell and gone following a particular ritual path, but her heart leapt. The green meant someone authorized to enter was waiting inside, and that was a list limited to Artie, Jenny... and Daniel. "Are you back?" she called, pushing her way inside, expecting to see Daniel, wondering if he'd be wearing any clothes.

Instead, Jenny Click stood by Marla's window, arms crossed over her chest, eyes puffy with sleeplessness or tears or both. "Marla," she said. "I'm back."

Something inside Marla's chest turned black and curled in on itself. "What happened?"

"Can we go up on the roof? I'm not doing so well with enclosed spaces after.... I didn't even take a plane home. I flew under my own power."

Marla took two plastic cups from her cabinet, a mostly-full bottle of bourbon—she didn't drink much, but it was good to have the stuff on hand—and said, "After you."

Up on the roof, beneath a gray autumnal sky, they sat in a couple of lawn chairs Marla had dragged up there. Marla poured out the liquor and handed Jenny a glass. She held it loosely, but didn't drink, staring off into the distance.

"Daniel's dead, isn't he?" Marla said.

Jenny nodded.

"Then why don't I feel an uncontrollable urge to avenge him? Shouldn't the geas have kicked in?" She was, desperately, hoping that Jenny was wrong. Daniel was hard to kill. His childhood alone was testament to that.

"Daniel was killed when the cavern under the ruins collapsed. You can't get revenge from rocks. But Rasmussen's the one who made the rocks fall. He's beyond our reach, though. He's dead dead, too." Jenny's voice was completely flat.

"Tell me about it," Marla said. Hoping she'd hear a loophole.

Jenny shook her head. "We waited. We watched. Rasmussen was there with a few apprentices. Eventually they took a boat out to the ruins, said some mystical stuff, and a doorway opened. They descended, and we followed, down about a hundred thousand stone steps. I'm not even exaggerating much. I stopped counting stairs after the first fifteen thousand, and that wasn't halfway. My ears popped as the pressure changed. Eventually we reached this giant cavern, who knows how far under the sea. There were torches on the walls, burning funny colors because the air down there was strange. The walls were dripping water, and there were all these paintings in red and vivid blue, primitive-looking pictures of eyes and stars and towers and who knows what all. There was a big pool in the floor, like a moon pool, and all Rasmussen's apprentices stood in a circle around it, pulled out knives, cut their own throats, and tumbled into the water. I don't know if they were willing sacrifices or mind-controlled or what… the water barely rippled when they went in. Barely rippled at all." She fell silent.

"And then?" Marla said.

Jenny took a small sip of her bourbon. "Rasmussen was chanting, and Daniel and I figured, this is it, right? No longer outnumbered, safe to strike. So we stepped in. I turned up my flame, and Daniel started sucking Rasmussen's life out. We weren't even trying to kill him—we aren't assassins—just distract him, mess up his ritual, ruin his plans like he ruined Artie's. But we were either too late, or the break in the ritual pissed off the creature Rasmussen was trying to summon, but…" She shook her head. "The water started to froth, white. And the dead apprentices climbed out, their robes dripping, and there were… they weren't tentacles, they were… filaments, umbilical cords, I don't know, these slimy ropes, running from the dead apprentices' backs, down into the water. Their eyes were black, their mouths hung open, but they still had their knives, and they were coming for us, and for Rasmussen too. So I started burning them, but they were so drenched it was hard, and Daniel was yelling about how they didn't *have* any life force, he couldn't do anything to stop them, and then Rasmussen just let out this… wail. The dead apprentices even stopped to look at him. Then Rasmussen said 'Ruined. All is ruined.'"

Jenny lifted her eyes to Marla. "And then Rasmussen raised his arms above his head, and spoke an incantation, and the cavern ceiling started to fall in on us. I grabbed Daniel's hand, and dragged him toward the stairs, but the rocks fell down, the doorway was blocked. The dead apprentices fell onto Rasmussen, hacking at him with their knives, but he caught my eye, and he smiled at me. Like he was glad, if he was going to die, that I was going to die, too."

"But you didn't die."

Jenny shook her head. "After that, everything's confused. The ceiling was falling in. There was no way out, nowhere to go, except the moon pool, even though we knew there was something under there, something that had taken control of the apprentices… but it was a choice between certain death and probable death. So we chose the latter. Daniel and I jumped in. There was a tunnel. We swam past those filaments—I had a spell to let me hold my breath for a long time, and Daniel could live without breathing—and we swam down, down, the pressure building, I thought we'd die. The apprentices were swimming down after us, too, one even touched my ankle. But finally the tunnel opened up, and it was just black water on all sides. And down below us, this red glow, like streaks of lava, and… something. Just the shape of something black, blacker than the deeps of the sea, and those filaments stretching down to the thing. And there were more filaments, loose ones, floating around like a kelp forest, and I knew if one touched me, I'd be dead. Or worse. I lost track of Daniel during the confusion. I swam up, not too fast, because I didn't know if I was deep enough to get the bends. I've never been so scared. Eventually, after a long time, I reached the surface." She shrugged. "Daniel never did."

Marla frowned. "How long did you wait?"

"Two days and two nights," she said. "Sitting in the ruins, just waiting. But he never came up."

"You didn't see him die, though," Marla said.

"You weren't there." Jenny's eyes were faraway again. "There was a god beneath us. An angry one. Rocks falling. The weight of all that water. The darkness. The dead, with knives, pursuing us. There was nothing but death in that place. Sometimes I'm not sure I really survived. Sometimes I think this is a dream."

"More a nightmare," Marla said.

"I was in love with him," Jenny said, her tone not changing at all, and Marla was so startled she almost spilled her drink.

"What?"

"In love. With Daniel. Always. From the moment I met him. But he never saw it. He thought of me like a sister." She shook her head. "He loved you. Only you." Jenny turned her face to Marla, narrowed her eyes, and said, "What the fuck is so wonderful about *you*?"

"Jenny, I—"

"No," she said. "I'm done."

And Jenny Click burst into flame.

Marla had seen her friend wrap herself in fire a hundred hundred times before, but this was different. This was no aura. This was all-consuming. Jenny was letting herself burn. Marla reached out to her, shouting a wordless cry of denial, and the flesh of her hand cracked and burned instantly. The cloak healed her, new flesh crawling up to cover the burns, but the pain was unimaginable, as if she'd plunged her arm into the sun. Marla stumbled back, tipping her chair over, the heat almost a wall pushing her back. She thought, *If I can get the cloak over Jenny, I can heal her,* but of course if Marla removed the cloak, she would be burned to cinders herself. Less than cinders. Just vapor and liberated gases.

Marla had no time to come up with a better idea. The flames flickered, and Jenny was gone, along with the chair she'd been sitting on, and the glass of bourbon she'd held. There was nothing left of Jenny Click but a few pale gray ashes, and when a wind blew, even the ashes floated away. Marla watched them go.

Chapter Fourteen

"**Do you really think Daniel is dead?**" Marla stared down as she swirled the brandy in her glass, watching the ripples, thinking of the sea.

"Hard to say," Artie said, absorbed in contemplation of his own drink. They were in the living room of his house in the cliff, a space that now seemed to echo with emptiness. "He can survive in tough conditions, but… old gods? Zombie apprentices? I don't know. And Jenny didn't give up on him easily. I'll send some people to poke around, see if the Bay Witch has any contacts down that way, but…" He shook his head.

"The sea is deep," Marla said.

Artie nodded. "So… how pissed at me are you?"

Marla considered. "About as pissed as I am at myself. You shouldn't have sent them. I should have gone along. I could have made a difference."

"Maybe. But you can't dwell on that. Let me be the one who dwells on failure here." He took a deep drink, though Marla didn't think you were supposed to quaff brandy, and wiped his mouth on his sleeve. "I think I'm done having apprentices."

"Oh?"

"Hurts too much to lose them," Artie said. "And Jenny… I should've known she had those feelings for Daniel. How'd I miss that?"

"Dunno what we could have done about it," Marla said. "Maybe talked. Maybe that would have helped." She shifted on the couch. "It did make me wonder about the geas, though. I mean, shouldn't we feel… something? With Daniel and Jenny both gone?"

"The geas won't trigger for suicide, and with Rasmussen gone, there's nobody to kill on Daniel's behalf. The geas is smart, its definitions are narrow—it only triggers if someone willfully murders one of us. If some guy accidentally hits me with a bus, you won't have to go murder the driver. Hell, if I came at you with a sword and you killed me in self-defense, the geas wouldn't trigger you to take revenge against *yourself*. The spell recognizes those kinds of complexities. Of course, if you just killed me because you felt like it, without cause, your brain would start to eat itself—you'd be stone crazy and dead by your own hand within a week."

"So at least we still have each other," Marla said, only a little ironically.

"If you can stand the sight of me," Artie said.

The doorbell rang. Artie frowned, hauling himself up off the couch. *Daniel?*, Marla thought, and rose to follow him.

Artie opened the door, and Ernesto was there.

"Artie. Marla. I'm so sorry. I just heard. I wasn't sure if I should come, but—"

"Get in here, you bastard," Artie growled, and for a little while, they were a family again, grieving together.

But that time passed.

"It's been six years," Marla said, sipping one of Juliana's specials. She made a face. "What the hell is this?"

Juliana drifted over to Marla's place at the bar, swabbed at the sticky surface with a damp rag, and shrugged. "Spring water and orphan's tears. You said you wanted something appropriate for grief."

It was never possible to tell if Juliana was kidding. She had the emotional range of a painting of a ghost. Marla put the glass down. "Six years," she said again. "Since my best friend died right in front of me. And six years and maybe three days since an even better friend died, very far away from me. I usually spend this day in bed thinking about things I hate and people I want to kick. But today? Today I have to work."

"A dollar is a dollar," Juliana said.

"I don't do it for the money," Marla said. "I do it for the power." She'd long since stopped doing jobs for cash, having squirreled away enough savings for her meager needs. These days, when she did jobs for Felport's sorcerers, she demanded payment in secrets and techniques. She'd learned a lot. Mostly ways to hurt people, and to avoid being hurt herself. "I need to see Rondeau," she said.

"He's not here." Juliana's eyes were watchful hollows under her thatch of orange hair.

Marla laced her fingers together and let her hands rest on the bar. "I've always appreciated your hospitality, Juliana. But I won't tolerate being lied to."

Juliana glanced at Marla, then down, to the silver pin that held Marla's white-and-purple cloak closed. "He's in back," Juliana said. "You scare him. He hides."

"I know. But I've already done the worst thing I'm ever going to do to him. It's all smooth sailing from there, comparatively." She picked up her shoulder bag carefully, so as not to disturb the fragile vessel inside, glass and fluid swaddled in old clothes. She went through the dim bar to the closet that led to the secret conference room, said the necessary magic words, and pushed inside.

Rondeau sat in a chair at the far end of the room, a dark-haired, dark-eyed Hispanic boy of maybe 16, so young—though that was the age Marla had been when she first met Artie, wasn't it? Rondeau was far deeper into the world of magic at this age than Marla had been. He did regular work for Hamil, helped out Juliana in the bar, had a lot of contacts on the street, was a dab hand with a butterfly knife, and even had some peculiar and unique magic of his own, presumably related to whatever weirdness allowed him to possess the body he called his own.

"Hey," Marla said. She opened up her bag and withdrew the oversized pickle jar of greenish fluid that held the preserved arc of Rondeau's original jaw. When he saw it, Rondeau's hand went automatically to his face, touching his chin, either for reassurance or protection. She hadn't needed to bring the jaw—it wouldn't even work in here—but she knew it would seize Rondeau's attention. "Your jaw spoke to me today. It told me you knew the haruspex."

"Haruspex?" His bewilderment, even veiled by fear, seemed genuine.

Marla considered. If questioned properly, the jaw spoke to her, and it knew whatever Rondeau did. Like subatomic particles that once collide and remain connected forever, regardless of distance, Rondeau shared information with his jaw instantaneously, against his will. Sometimes the jaw even knew things before Rondeau did, an oddity that Marla accepted but did not understand.

"A haruspex divines the future by studying the arrangement of entrails," she said. He looked blank. "Intestines. Guts, Rondeau."

His eyes widened. "Him? The Belly Killer? That's why he's doing it?" He swore, an inhuman obscenity that made Marla wince. Cursing was his particular power. If he'd uttered those syllables outside the conference room's protective walls, paint would have blistered and flies dropped dead, and Marla would have endured ringing in her ears for hours afterward. "That makes a little more sense, motive-wise. Not much, but a little."

"Tell me," Marla said.

"You don't want to know. I told Carlton Spandau, and you heard what happened to him."

"Victim number six. Is the killer someone I know? Someone Carlton knew?"

"He's a nobody." Rondeau shrugged. "Never been an apprentice, never witnessed anything magical…" He shook his head. "Carlton hired me to track the guy down, and after the fifth killing, I found him. Until three months ago, the killer was just an ordinary guy with a lousy job. Then… something happened. Something that made him strong enough to kill Carlton, Mangrove, Sorenson… I don't know what, but when I tracked him leaving the murder scene, I smelled, I dunno, ozone, electricity."

Marla blinked. "Like the Thrones? The way they smell?"

He looked away. "I don't know. Maybe. I don't want any part of it, though. Way above my pay grade."

How could the Thrones be involved in the serial murder of some of Felport's most prominent sorcerers? The Thrones were just… annoyances. Self-aggrandizing supernatural pigeons. It didn't make sense. "I want to find the guy," Marla said. "Sauvage is offering a big reward."

"I can tell you what I know," Rondeau said slowly, "But you have to keep my name out of it, and I'll want something in return."

"I'm reasonable. Besides, maybe the Belly Killer will gut me, and you'll be done with me forever." She grinned.

He looked wounded. "If you died, who would take care of my jaw?" He gave her an address, and Marla put the jaw away. "Be seeing you."

As soon as she stepped outside the magic-nullifying confines of the conference room, her head rang like a bell, and she staggered and fell to her knees, barely keeping a grip on her bag. The roaring noise in her head resolved itself to a shout, in a familiar voice—Artie's voice.

It said, "I'm dead, I'm DEAD, get the fucker who killed me, you hear me, get him, get him, I'm DEAD, he cut me open and I'm DEAD."

"Oh, fuck," Marla whispered, clutching her head. "The Belly Killer got Artie." And then, more loudly: "Artie. I'm on it. I'm already after him."

"Good," the voice said, and then, in her head, there was blessed silence, broken only by her own racing thoughts.

But unless she avenged Artie, the voice would be back.

Marla went to Artie's house, just in case he'd been a victim of someone or something else, but, no: it was the Belly Killer again, the mysterious man who'd left black-flecked entrails piled messily in a succession of front yards, alleyways, and darkened houses. A man who'd killed sorcerers, men who should have been able to defend themselves. The victims had been low-level people at first, but more recently included members of the ruling council: first Sorenson, and now, poor Artie.

Ernesto was there, looking down at the body, doubtless preparing a report for the chief sorcerer, Sauvage. "Marla," he said. "You don't need to look at this—"

"I need to know all I can," she said, pushing past him. Artie had been on his couch, reading a magazine. The Belly Killer had opened him up, stirred around his insides, left them hanging messily. The corpse on the couch looked nothing like her mentor, her friend, the man who'd given her a life. Artie hadn't managed immortality after all. She looked at Ernesto. "I have to find the killer. The geas."

"Shit," Ernesto said. "Of course, I didn't think... Let me know if there's anything I can do, any resource I can give you, to help find this guy. And know we're all searching, too. Sauvage made it a priority."

"I've got a lead," Marla said. "I'll follow it." She nodded toward Artie. "He'll never let me rest until I kill the killer."

Ernesto nodded. "Sauvage's reward is good whether the Belly Killer is dead or alive."

"Guess we know which one it will be," Marla said.

Marla followed Rondeau's lead to an antique store called Jacob's Jumble, one of those cramped downtown shops that replenished itself ghoulishly from estate sales and contentious divorces. Supposedly the Belly Killer worked here, which made Marla wonder if he'd found some object of power—maybe he'd been possessed by an enchanted knife used in some long-ago sorcerer's vendetta. Or maybe he'd found an artifact. Such discoveries weren't unprecedented, as Marla knew.

The store's name was written in flaking gold and black paint on a dirty glass door, and she pushed in, murmuring a little spell to silence the bell above the door. Buzzing fluorescent tubes lit the crowded shelves, and a trebly radio played the last notes of a Beach Boys song somewhere deeper in the shop. There was a glass counter full of old tin toys, and a stool behind it, and a cash register, but no one was watching the till.

The place smelled of dust and grease, but not electricity. She carefully checked all the aisles—there weren't that many—and even looked inside a battered old wardrobe, just in case. She pushed open a door marked "Employee's Only"—that stupid apostrophe made her grit her teeth—but it was empty back there, too, just a dim storeroom filled with unsorted merchandise; it didn't look much different from the front of the store, really. A red fire door stood half open, though, propped with a brick, and she stepped through into a graffitied alleyway behind the shop. No sign of anyone... but there was a cat, freshly dead, resting on the rear steps. Marla looked at its small pale intestines, which had been pulled out of its body and spread out on the concrete steps. Had the killer seen some portent of her arrival in the arrangement of the entrails, and fled? If he could get information like that from a cat, what did the spilled guts of humans—or sorcerers—tell him?

"You *missed* him, he's *gone*," Artie's voice—or the ghostly recording of his voice, or the geas imitating his voice—grumbled in her mind.

"Shit," she said, and decided to return to Juliana's. In the secret conference room, Artie's voice couldn't reach her, and she could think about what to do next in peace. She could always squeeze Rondeau a little harder and see if any more information came out, too.

Juliana's bar was dark and empty, which wasn't surprising, as it was early in the day, but her door was always open to sorcerers. As far as anyone could tell, Juliana never slept. She never seemed entirely awake, either, though. "Juliana?" Marla called. She wanted Rondeau, but there was no way he'd come if she called.

Something moaned from the direction of the bar. Marla hesitated near the door. She didn't want to interrupt Juliana in the middle of her ugly delights. Apart from her unwillingness to see such a thing—whatever it might be—who knew what consequences would befall Juliana if her act went uncompleted? "It's me, Marla. I need to talk to you. Are you... I don't know... decent?"

Another moan, weaker this time, and then Marla caught the smell of ozone, but not the pure scent she associated with the Thrones. Similar, but threaded with a whiff of corruption, like a fried power transformer dropped in a sewer. She rushed toward the bar, holding her cloak like bat's wings, prepared to clothe herself in purple at the slightest threat.

She didn't find the Belly Killer, but she found his work. Juliana lay behind the bar, shirtless and bloodied, trying to push her intestines back inside.

"Death," Juliana whispered, blood spotting her thin lips. Her pupils were huge, nearly obscuring her irises.

"Wait." Marla started to take off her cloak—it could heal Juliana—but then she hesitated. What if the Belly Killer was here, lurking, waiting for Marla to drop her defenses? What if Juliana had been left alive as a trap? Marla didn't want to end up with her own belly unzipped.

"His death," Juliana said, gesturing at her unspooled insides. "You... He saw..." Her eyes fluttered.

Fuck it. Marla could take care of herself, cloak or not. She unhooked the clasp at her throat—

But too late. Juliana died, eyes wide open, and Marla cursed. She'd let fear make her hesitate. Not again.

Marla stood, reversing her cloak with a mental command. Ruthless strength and a desire for violence filled her. She smiled, fear diminishing in a surge of power, and with her heightened senses she scanned the room, she felt for life, but there was no one but herself, not upstairs, not down here, not—wait. A throbbing absence. A place even her potent new senses could not penetrate. The conference room. She threw open the closet door—seeing easily through the feeble illusion of a broom closet—and rushed inside.

Rondeau screamed and huddled under the table, covering his head and whimpering.

As soon as Marla crossed the threshold, her cloak reversed itself, the dark, maniacal strength leaving her. Of course. Her artifact's power was useless here. A good thing. She hated to think what might have happened to Rondeau. A quick, professional glance assured Marla that no one else occupied the room.

"Get up, Rondeau," she said, tired. "I'm not going to hurt you."

"That stink of electricity." Marla sipped a cold glass of water. Her voice seemed unnaturally loud in the empty bar. "That's what I don't get."

Rondeau sat across from her, a plate of cold nachos before him. He stirred a mound of guacamole with a chip, wrinkling his nose. "You said it yourself. Smells like the Thrones."

"It doesn't make any sense." She tore a napkin into small pieces, thinking hard. "The Thrones watch. That's all they do."

"That's all they've done *so far*," Rondeau said. "Not the same thing."

"Point. But even if the Thrones made a practice of killing people, the Belly Killer isn't one of them, he's just a normal man, and anyway, the smell isn't quite right. So what's going on?" Marla was frustrated. She wasn't a detective. She was a leg-breaker.

"If he's a haruspex, reading the future in guts… then what's he see? What's he looking for?"

Marla shook her head. "I don't know. I'll ask before I kill him, though." She dropped bits of torn napkin into her glass and watched them darken, soaking up water. "We have to find him. Want to come with me?"

"Ah. I shouldn't. I need to stay here. See to Juliana." They'd wrapped her up in a tarp, but that was hardly a final resting place. "And… this place is mine now. Juliana made arrangements, if she died, for me to take over. But we didn't think she'd die of… this."

Marla stared at him. She hadn't thought about who would take possession of the bar, and, more importantly, the conference room, where the city's sorcerers preferred to do their darkest business and take their most secret meetings. It was a valuable inheritance. "Were you two lovers?"

"I don't know that love had anything to do with it. We were close."

Marla nodded. "So, ah… am I still welcome here?"

Rondeau looked at her for a long time. "You never said you were sorry. For what you did to me, when I was little. Hamil told me you were, but…"

"You're right," Marla said. "You're right." She took a deep breath. "I'm sorry. If I had it to do over again, I wouldn't. And, I know it's not really any excuse, but…" She held up an edge of the cloak. "I wasn't entirely myself that day."

"Okay," Rondeau said. "Then you're still welcome here."

Stop socializing! Artie's shade snapped. *Avenge me!*

"I'd better go," she said.

"Good luck."

Marla trudged through the bar with her head down, thinking about what leads she could run down next. She went up the steps to street level and turned down an alleyway, toward Hamil's place. Maybe he'd have some ideas.

"Hiya," someone said. Marla lifted her head, startled, and the smell of ozone and half-digested food filled her nostrils. Something hit her on the side of the head, impossibly fast, and she caught a glimpse of pockmarked cheeks and greasy black hair, a figure moving fast as hummingbird wings. Her hair stood on end, crackling with sparks, and the strength suddenly ran out of her limbs like water from a broken pot.

I'm dead, I'm dead, she thought, trying to flip her cloak, but her numb mind wouldn't cooperate—her mental energy had been sapped as quickly as her physical strength. This was how he'd done it, then, how he'd killed such accomplished sorcerers—hitting hard, fast, somehow draining them of power. She was on the ground now, staring up, and he was standing over her, a thin, short man, nothing special, but special enough.

Dead, she thought, and she'd never know why, or what future the killer would read in her steaming remains.

Blackness came. Then, like bright flashes penetrating her closed eyelids, brilliant geysers of pain.

Chapter Fifteen

MARLA FLOATED IN A SPACE the color of wet newsprint, the air around her hissing like static. Was she dead? Was this her crappy afterlife?

Presences manifested, coalescing out of the static.

Thrones. Three identical, derelict men with fright-wig hair, dressed in cast-offs: suspenders, untucked flannel shirts, cotton pants fraying at the seams. They hovered, bobbing slightly, electricity crackling around them, eyes wide and luminous. They wore their human bodies badly, unable to conceal the light inside.

They spoke in concert, haltingly: "You... Death... His death..." Repeating Juliana's last words, and Marla wondered if this was pure hallucination, a last firing of synapses before the Belly Killer finished her off.

Then the Thrones inhaled together and spoke clearly, still in concert. "You must help us. Our agent has slipped from our control. We gave him power to act as our instrument, but he kills for his own reasons."

"Oh, you are shitting me," she said, and they winced. "The Belly Killer's working for you?"

"We... our duty... we... our obligation... We can only observe your kind until..." A pause, a clicking sound like a bolt sliding shut. "... a later date. We chose a servant to act for us on Earth, since we cannot intervene directly, but he no longer heeds us. Once given, our powers cannot be withdrawn. We may not—we may not—we may not move against him directly. You must stop him."

Marla sensed a note of desperation. Did the Thrones report to a higher power? If so, were they trying to cover up their mistake, throw her at the problem, and hope for the best?

What the hell. She was trying to stop the Killer *anyway*. She still said, "What's in it for me?"

"If you help us, you will be... absolved."

"That's reassuring," she said. "How about some practical, tactical help? I wouldn't mind being able to spit lightning and sap strength like he does.

"We cannot trust you with such power," the Thrones said. "We made that mistake once. Mortals make poorer vessels than we supposed. You lack pure motives. Given strength, our agent killed recklessly. Given the power of divination, he became obsessed with personal matters."

Marla wondered what he was divining. Stock market trends? The winners of horse races? "You have to give me something, here, guys."

"We will give you a small gift. Not strength, not power, but... something." They flickered, fading out. "Stop him, and we will absolve you." They blended with the static, finally disappearing entirely.

"Absolve yourselves, assholes," she said to the emptiness. The static darkened to black.

Marla woke to pain. Not her stomach, which felt whole, but her face. She pushed herself up, and black spots of agony swam before her eyes like gorged flies. She tried to whisper a painkilling spell, but something was wrong with her mouth. She was on the table in a brightly-lit, antiseptic room, all chrome and porcelain. Torture chamber?

Rondeau appeared in the doorway, in the company of a thin, serious-looking man in a lab coat, wearing little round glasses. He seemed familiar, but Marla couldn't place him, because she couldn't think, because she *hurt*.

"Shit, she's awake," Rondeau said.

"She's strong," the other man said. "That's good." And then the man was beside her. "You're hurt. This will help you rest." He held a hypodermic needle.

Marla tried to say "No!" but her mouth still didn't work, and she reached up to touch her chin, but instead her fingers went too far, and sank into softness, and she screamed. Her jaw was gone. A moment later everything went black, from the pain or the needle or both, and either way, she welcomed it.

Marla woke in a hospital bed. Her jaw ached, but—

She sat up and touched her chin. Opened her mouth, experimentally, and it all seemed to work, though it was aching, and tender, and the teeth didn't feel right.

"Hey, you're up," Rondeau said, walking in. "How's the new jaw?"

"How did you... do this?" she said.

"You know Langford, the biomancer? I brought you to his place when I found you because he's the closest thing to a doctor I know. He got you hooked up to an IV, replenished your fluids, stuff like that. He also took some of your skin cells and accelerated their growth, made new skin crawl over a framework of titanium or something."

"So this isn't my jaw? I'm, what, a cyborg now?"

Rondeau snorted. "Well, turns out Langford did all that work for nothing, because during the night, while the new skin was growing, that cloak of yours somehow *grew you a new jaw*. That's some serious mojo you're working, Marla. Langford came in this morning to do the surgery, attach the new jaw to your face, and saw it wasn't necessary. Says you owe him for the new jaw anyway though. And you can keep it as a spare."

Marla nodded. "Thanks for helping me, Rondeau." She wouldn't have died without him, not with the cloak's magic, but if some mugger had rolled her and stolen the cloak off her back...

He shrugged. "I was just walking by, saw you in the street, what, I was going to leave you?"

"After what I did to you, it would've been understandable."

He grinned. "Well, to be honest, I *did* feel a little warm fuzzy at seeing you got *your* jaw ripped off. What happened?"

"The Belly Killer. But why my jaw instead of my guts?"

"Maybe he wants to keep tabs on you. Hell, if he knows how, he can make the jaw tell him anything and everything you know, right? And use it to keep tabs on you."

"Yeah. I was afraid it might be something like that."

"You'll be going after him," Rondeau said. "I just want you to know, I'll help you."

"I don't know if there's anything you can do." She swung her legs off the bed, feeling a little shaky, but not too bad. She followed Rondeau out the door, into the clean room—Langford's lab, she supposed. The biomancer was there, examining Juliana's corpse, which rested on his exam table, her guts coiled neatly to one side.

"The patient awakes," Langford said, barely glancing up from his work. "How are you feeling?"

Marla didn't answer. She stared at Juliana, or more properly at her intestines coiled beside her, a meaningless spill of gray, like the alphabet disarranged.

But *only* disarranged. She could read the letters of that alphabet, just not the mussed message.

"The tapes," she said, turning to Rondeau. "We have to go to the bar, to the office, and looked at the security tapes."

"You're the boss," Rondeau said.

Juliana's security equipment was surprisingly high-tech, and Rondeau knew how to run it, so soon Marla was peering at a frozen image of Juliana's spilled guts in their original, portentous configuration.

Marla could read the message there. The Thrones had given her the gift of haruspicy. Not quite as impressive as the ability to sap strength and spit lightning, but it was something.

Except the thing she was reading in Juliana's intestines was *bullshit*.

"I can read this," she told Rondeau. "It says I'm the Belly Killer's only chance at survival. Except I've got every intention of killing him."

"You're a woman of many talents," Rondeau said. "That explains why the guy didn't kill you—might explain why he took your jaw, too. If you were my only hope, I'd want to keep track of you, too."

Marla rubbed her chin, her sense of violation returning. The Belly Killer could find out anything she knew. Of course, he had to ask the right questions, but he was practiced in divination, so he probably could.

"You know," Rondeau said, "I can still feel my jaw." He pointed east, in the general direction of Marla's apartment. "I could walk straight to it, I bet." He grinned.

Marla stared at him, then concentrated, trying to feel... There. To the west.

She grinned back at him.

Ernesto had investigated the earlier murders—once they realized they had a supernatural serial killer on their hands—and he sent over the crime scene photos. It didn't take her long to discern the Belly Killer's theme.

"So what does the future hold?" Rondeau asked, straining for casualness. "Cataclysm? Alien invasion? Are hemlines dropping this spring?"

Marla shook her head, her own hopes for a grand revelation already gone. The killer was interested in the merely personal, as the Thrones had said. "The Belly Killer doesn't care about that. His divinations have one purpose: To find out the details of his own death."

Rondeau gaped. "That's it? He killed Sorenson and Mann and Chandler to find out how he's going to die?

"What else matters?" Marla asked.

Marla walked west, thinking. The Belly Killer read the future, and those readings spelled out a multitude of possible deaths. He'd seen futures where he died at Sorenson's hands, Chandler's, Artie's, all his victims, and still more who hadn't been killed yet, who the Belly Killer would surely target soon. Artie Mann's entrails named Juliana as a threat, and so the Belly Killer took steps to remove her. Marla couldn't imagine Juliana hurting anyone—unless they tried to get into the conference room without permission.

The weight of the rifle hanging on its strap over her shoulder shifted uncomfortably.

The Belly Killer did what no ancient priestly haruspex had ever done. He attempted to change the future, eliminating risks and reading the new future in the guts of the old. As a result of those murders, every sorcerer in the city was gunning for him now. If he hadn't killed his first sorcerer, the city's secret masters might never have noticed him, but now he'd trapped himself in a snare of recursive causality. But why the hell did Juliana's guts name Marla as his salvation? She *had* to kill him—it wasn't optional. The geas demanded it.

She turned down a side street, homing in on her missing piece, her torn-off jaw broadcasting like a communications tower engaged in the transmission of pain.

After another hour of walking, she found the Killer in the parking lot of dead supermarket. Newspaper covered the building's windows and half the letters in the store's sign were missing. A single shopping cart lay upside-down in the center of the yellow-lined lot like the skeleton of an exotic dinosaur. The big mercury lights didn't work, as defunct as the store itself, but Marla's eyes could do wonders with the moon and starlight.

She settled, invisible, in the shadow of rusty dumpster full of jagged wood, remnant of some attempt at reconstruction. She watched the Belly Killer, who stood in the center of the parking lot, hands at his sides, Marla's bloody jaw tucked carelessly into his back pocket like a boy's slingshot.

Hard to miss at this distance, she thought, quietly slinging the rifle over her shoulder. She wasn't much of a shootist, but her brother had taught her the basics of handling a long gun, and from here she was confident of her ability to put a bullet in the Belly Killer's head. He'd turned her arms and legs to sacks of concrete last time, so lethal action at a distance was the more prudent choice.

A long dark car purred into the parking lot, and Marla lowered her gun. What was this?

The front doors opened and two burly men in ill-fitting suits got out, moving off to either side to flank the Killer. The car's back door opened, and a stout, well dressed man got out. Marla recognized him instantly. Sauvage, the chief sorcerer, a man with a reptile's patience and no tolerance for fools.

Marla had read his name in the remains of Sorenson's corpse.

"Let's see it," Sauvage said.

The Belly Killer nodded and took the jawbone from his back pocket, holding it up.

Mine, Marla thought fiercely, leaning forward. Why would Sauvage want her jaw? He knew she existed, she had a certain reputation, but—

"That's not Cochran's jaw," Sauvage said flatly.

The Belly Killer giggled, a long, weird titter.

It was a trick, a lure to bring Sauvage into the open. Cochran was Sauvage's chief rival, so of course he'd come personally for the man's jaw— his necromancers could interrogate it for all kinds of secrets. Marla hadn't even heard Cochran was dead—the Belly Killer was keeping himself occupied.

Sauvage waved his hand and the goons lunged for the Belly Killer, who still held up the jawbone like a proud child displaying a lumpy ashtray made in arts and crafts. One of the thugs struck the Killer solidly, knocking him over. Marla winced as her jawbone fell. Sauvage bent and picked it up, turning it in his hands. The goons aimed kicks at the Belly Killer's stomach.

The air changed, becoming heavier, crackling, reeking, and the Belly Killer sparkled with greasy light. Tentacles lashed out, pure energy gleaming like razorwire, and slit the goons' stomachs deftly, spilling their secrets to the asphalt as they fell to their knees, looks of stupid surprise on their faces. The Belly Killer regained his feet and peered down at their guts.

All this happened in an instant, before even Sauvage could react. Marla lifted her rifle, but the Killer was still sparkling with electricity, and she suspected any projectile that hit his aura would vaporize.

Damn it, she was going to have to fly. She *hated* flying.

Marla dropped the rifle, murmured the ritual insult to gravity, and her body was propelled skyward. With a wrenching twist she got control of her trajectory, arrowing down toward Sauvage, hooking her hands under his fleshy armpits, hauling him into the air without looking back, straining under the weight. She imagined the Belly Killer streaking through the sky after her like a comet, like malevolent ball lightning, and made herself go faster—but the Killer didn't follow. He was still reading the guts. Hell, maybe he was finding out her destination in them.

Sauvage, surprisingly calm for a man hurtling through the air away from near-certain death, said, "Marla, right? Thanks for the assist. Care to tell me what you were doing back there?"

"Of course. If you make sure not to drop that jaw."

Rondeau surprised her again by not arguing. "Sure. Count me in." He took Sauvage aside, making him a drink from the private stock in Juliana's office. No, his office, Marla reminded herself. Rondeau even acted like he belonged there, like he'd inhabited the space for years.

Marla examined her jaw critically. Scraped, bloody, the gums already drawing back from the teeth. An incisor cracked, and a canine missing entirely. Still, even damaged and redundant, it felt good to have her missing piece back. She wrapped it in a handkerchief and tucked it into Rondeau's wall safe.

"How long before he gets here?" Sauvage swirled ice in his empty glass.

"I'm not sure. If he can fly like a Throne—"

"Time enough for another drink, at least," Sauvage said, and turned back to the liquor cabinet. He handed Marla a glass, and lifted his own. "Sorry for your loss, Marla. To Artie. He was a filthy old fuck, but I liked him."

"Hear hear," Marla said. "And ditto."

Rondeau hung a handwritten "Closed for Renovations" sign on the front door to keep customers away, and Sauvage and Rondeau took up residence inside the magic-nullifying conference room. "You could just stay in here, too," Rondeau said. "Why take the risk of hitting Mr. Lightning-face head on?"

Marla shook her head. "Can't make it look too easy—the Belly Killer might suspect a trap. We should make at least a pretense of protecting Sauvage." Really, she just wanted another shot at the guy. He'd sucker punched her last time, and besides taking her jaw, he'd dinged her pride, too.

She left the conference room—leaving the door ajar—and leaned against the wall facing the door, waiting.

Half an hour later, the door swung open, and the Killer entered, giggling.

He was short and scrawny, with greasy black hair hanging past his ears. Pockmarks made braille of his face, and he grinned crookedly, teeth speckled with green and yellow, and similar stains covered his white t-shirt and frayed khakis. Nevertheless, there was about him that sense of power, of crackling electricity, and the smell of lightning in the air. He giggled almost spastically, a vocal tic. "Sauvage. He's here. Let me have him."

"How about I just tear you to into fun-sized pieces instead?"

He shook his head. "You won't. You're my salvation."

"We'll see about that," she said, and reversed her cloak.

The Belly Killer took a step forward, and the energies surrounding him became visible, white primary shapes rotating and revolving. A fire-spoked wheel. A translucent blue ball of lightning. A coruscating pinwheel, spinning wildly around his head. He lifted his foot, sparks crackling from the sole of his sneaker to the floor like lightning streaking to earth from a thunderhead. The Killer licked his lips, blue fire sparking where his tongue touched. "We can be friends. I'll tell you secrets. Important things."

Marla looked on him through the eyes of the cloak's alien intelligence—a gaze of weights and measures—and came to a conclusion: *Overconfidence.* The Belly Killer had never been beaten, or even bloodied. But he'd never faced something like her before. Marla launched herself at him, claws of shadow sheathing her hands.

The Killer giggled, and waved his hand, and Marla felt a faint tingle in her limbs—he was trying to sap her strength again, but the attack slid off the cloak's defenses.

His eyes widened, and he gasped. A net of flashing light wrapped around Marla and caught her in mid-air. She clawed through, teeth snapping, mouth full of spectral fangs. The Belly Killer's fiery lace parted under her onslaught and she scrambled at him, snarling.

He shouted "No!" and, in his surprise, he simply kicked at her. He might as well have kicked a buzz saw; he drew back his foot, howling, having lost his shoe and most of a toe. Marla tossed the shredded remains of both aside and went for his throat.

Remembering his power, the Killer struck with glowing tentacles and hurled her aside. She hit the wall, bounced, and shot to her feet, going for him again.

He grunted, throwing up a barrier, and Marla clambered over, heedless of the burning damage done to her hands. The cloak would heal her—the pain was meaningless. Moreover, he wasn't trying to strike with lethal force, because he thought she was going to *save* him somehow!

She came over his barrier, clawing for his face, and pinned him to the ground. "Mine," she said, and the purple even changed her voice, made it a low and dusky growl of menace. Marla raised a hand gauntleted in razored shadows.

"Daniel," the Killer said, his reeking breath on her face, and Marla paused.

Kill him, the cloak whispered in her head, and "Kill him! Kill the fucker now!" Artie Mann's voice shouted with it, but Marla hesitated.

She reversed her cloak, because she wouldn't be able to stop from killing him if she remained in the purple. She closed her hands around his throat, but loosely. "What. About. Daniel."

"I saw. In Cochran's guts. I asked how to make you help me. The guts told me, 'Daniel.'" The Belly Killer grinned. "He's alive," the last word in singsong, "uhh-LIE-vuh."

"Where? How?"

"Ask me tomorrow," he said, and then flung Marla across the room on a sparking surge of lightning.

When Marla came to, groggy but—thanks to the cloak's healing power—not dead, Artie was howling at her. "You HAD him, you let him GO, you're going to pay for this, you can't—"

"Shut up," she muttered, and when she entered the conference room, his voice cut off in mid curse.

Sauvage stood holding the baseball bat in one casual hand. Rondeau prodded the Belly Killer's unconscious body with his foot. "Worked just like we wanted," Sauvage said. "He came in here all spitting plasma, but as soon as he crossed the threshold, pfft. Magic go bye-bye. I just cracked him across the head with the bat."

"He's not dead," Marla said. If he had been, Artie's ghost wouldn't have been screaming at her.

"Not yet. You can do the honors. Slice open his guts, see what the future holds, if you want."

Marla hesitated. Should she? Cut him open, and try to divine whatever it was he knew about Daniel? But what if it didn't work? Divination was tricky, you had to ask exactly the right questions in exactly the right way. And if she didn't get an answer she could use in the killer's guts, what then? Would *she* start stalking alleyways, cutting up hobos to find the answers? This was about *Daniel*. It had been years, and she'd done a good job of burying her pain and loss in work and violence, but if he was alive, if there was a chance he might come back to her... She couldn't trust herself not to descend into a dark and ugly obsession.

Which left the other option.

"He can be useful to you," Marla said. "I mean, a captive haruspex? Keep him in a cage somewhere, use him for... whatever. Lottery numbers. You know?"

"What about your geas?" Sauvage said.

Marla did her best to shrug nonchalantly. "You know. I can deal with it. There are ways to break a binding like that, right? Even when one of the parties is dead?"

"Sure, but they take a long time," Sauvage said. "Months, maybe years if the geas is strong enough. Even in the best cases, there's still a low murmur, like obscene tinnitus. And the rituals don't always work. I'm not saying I couldn't use a pocket prophet, but..." He nudged the body with his foot. "You sure?"

"I'm sure," Marla said. "I just... can I meet with the Killer tomorrow? Ask him a question?"

"Ah," Sauvage said. "Good, there's an ulterior motive. That's reassuring. It's okay, I don't care about the details. I respect secrets. Sure. Come by my place tomorrow, you can interrogate him." He cleared his throat. "You can also, you know. Start working for me."

Marla looked up from the Belly Killer, to Sauvage. "Really? For you, directly?"

"You showed me some stuff tonight," he said. "I want you on my payroll. Personal legbreaker and aide-de-camp. Assuming you can cope with Artie screaming in the back of your head. You interested?"

"Hell yes," Marla said.

"Now we've got that all settled," Rondeua said, "Can we get the greasy fucker out of my club?"

"One thing." Sauvage squatted down and tore open the Belly Killer's shirt, exposing his pale and pimply back. He drew a dagger, the hilt wrapped in red and black bands of electrical tape, and spat on the blade. Then, deftly, he cut a complex design into the Killer's flesh, making him stir and moan. "Nullification by scarification," Sauvage said. "Cut a grounding spell right into his flesh. Maybe his line into the Thrones' power source is cut off now, but better safe. Belt and suspenders, right? This'll keep him from using any zappy powers once we get out of here."

"What about his power to read the future in guts?" Rondeau said. "Will he lose that?"

"Doubtful," Sauvage said. "Power is one thing, and knowledge is something else. Spitting lightning, that's power. Reading portents, that's knowledge. It's hard to take away knowledge once it's imparted. Not impossible, of course. We can do amazing things to people's brains. It's easier to take knowledge away than put it in, though, or I'd be able to speak French and fix cars a lot better than I do."

Marla was examining the Killer's new scar, which seemed to twist as she looked at it. "You know how to draw runes like that, what, just off the top of your head?"

"That's why I'm chief sorcerer," Sauvage said. "Also: magic knife. For that matter, magic spit. It helps." He picked up the Belly Killer, slung the man's body over his shoulder, and said, "See you tomorrow."

Marla dropped into one of the room's chairs. She didn't hurt—the cloak had healed her injuries—but she was tired.

"Artie's ghost is going to plague you," Rondeau said after a moment. "It could take months, years, to dissolve the geas."

"You're not contributing to my general feeling of triumph here, Rondeau," she said.

"I just wanted to say, if it gets too bad, and you can't stand it, you can come to this room. Get a little break from the noise. Free of charge."

Marla stood up, and put her hand on his shoulder. She didn't kiss him, but she thought about it. "Thanks, Rondeau. I appreciate that."

She left the room, and as soon as she cleared the doorway, Artie Mann's voice hit her like a hammer, making her wince. "_ bitch, you swore, you promised to avenge me, you'll never sleep again, you'll suffer—"

And then his voice stopped abruptly, with a click like a deadbolt turning. She heard a many-throated hum, an irritatingly dramatic celestial chorus, which quickly faded.

A Throne stepped out of the darkness, ragged and disheveled as always. "Absolution," it said, lips not moving. "As promised. Your geas will not trouble you."

"Shit," she said, marveling at the silence in her head. "I guess you weirdos have some real power after all. Power to do something other than just fuck up, I mean."

"We have been... called away," it said. "Called... home. For... discipline. For our hubris. Our mistake. We will no longer be... observing... in this city."

"Don't let the pearly gates hit you in the ass on the way in," she said, and strolled toward the door, not even bothering to watch the Throne disappear.

Absolution, she thought. She'd accumulate new sins soon enough, she knew, but in the meantime she'd enjoy the unaccustomed lightness of grace. Maybe even add to it, a little, by giving Rondeau his jaw back. If she needed to get information from him in the future, she could just ask, couldn't she?

And tomorrow. Tomorrow she'd talk to that giggling bastard and find out what he knew about Daniel.

Chapter Sixteen

SAUVAGE HAD A PENTHOUSE APARTMENT furnished with over-stuffed couches, overflowing bookshelves, and oversized works of art, including a Jackson Pollack painting about the size of a garage door. Lots of the furniture had been shoved aside to make room for a large steel cage, which held the Belly Killer, a pile of blankets, and a bucket.

"The Killer's detoxing," Sauvage said. "From being an *asshole.*" He puffed on a fat cigar, which smelled foul, though at least the odor helped cover up the stink of the Belly Killer, who sat tittering and rocking in one corner of the cage. Not for the first time, Marla thought that Sauvage was a lot like Artie, minus the barely-concealed streak of profound insecurity. "Anyway," Sauvage said, "I'll give you some privacy. Just be careful he doesn't throw his poop at you. Yesterday he shoots lightning, today he throws poop. You gotta admire the spirit." He sauntered off deeper into his apartment.

Marla crossed her arms and leaned on the arm of a couch, looking in at the Belly Killer, who was humming to himself. "Speak, freak," she said.

"You did save my life," he said, not looking up. "I *told* you."

"So now tell me about Daniel."

"Okey dokey doke. Daniel's deep deep in the sea, he was deep deep asleep, hibernating like a bear, dormant like a volcano, but now he's wakey-wakey and on his way."

"What woke him—shit. The geas. Artie's death. Of course." She shook her head. "I saved you short-term, Mr. Giggles. Once Daniel gets here, he's going to have to kill you. And I'll help."

"I've seen a lot of ways I might die," the Killer said, shrugging. "We'll see, we'll see, we'll see."

"How long before he gets here?"

"A year, I fear, before he's here. The ocean's a big place. He's got a long walk ahead of him, a lot of water over his head."

Marla frowned. A *year*? "Maybe I should just kill you now, spare him the agony of Artie's ghost yelling at him."

"And maybe without the geas driving him and riding him and pushing him and pulling him he'll just sink back into the mud asleep." The Killer giggled. "Care to try?"

"No."

"I knew you'd say that." He winked, rather grotesquely.

"I can go look for him, though." Marla said. "Find him, help him, give him a ride home."

"The sea is big, and you are small. The future is a messy place, possibles branching out of possibles, but there's no future where you find him in the water. He'll come walking up out of the bay in ten or twelve or fourteen months. You'll just wait."

"Once he gets back here, you're dead."

The Killer giggled again, and picked up his bucket, and Marla managed to dive behind the couch before he could douse her with its contents, though the smell of the spatter was still horrible.

"Promises, promises," the Killer—the Giggler, now, more like—said.

Working for Sauvage opened up a whole new world for Marla. She was there when the new sorcerer's council was convened, since the Killer had eliminated a few of the previous members. Ernesto was brought in to fill Artie Mann's seat, while Gregor was promoted to take over from his mentor Cochran. They decided to leave Sorenson's seat empty and limit membership to nine people, so they could have an odd number of voting members and actually make decisions by majority rule, instead of getting stuck in deadlock, as had happened so many times before.

The Chamberlain, Viscarro, and Susan Wellstone lorded their seniority over the new members a bit, but Sauvage and Hamil were welcoming. Granger and the Bay Witch retained their positions, but they didn't take part in council meetings much anyway, and abstained from pretty much any vote that didn't impinge directly on their domains of city park and bay respectively.

Marla had entertained some hope of being promoted to the council herself, but her disappointment was short-lived, because it became apparent to her that Sauvage was grooming her for *something*—perhaps to be his successor. Running the city. It was a nice thought. Marla didn't mind hierarchical systems, as long as she was up somewhere near the top of them.

She did her work, she learned from the best, she got to know Sauvage as well as anybody could, probably... but in the back of her head, there was always Daniel.

A few times she went down to Sauvage's basement, where the Giggler had been relocated, trying to get more answers out of him. He always claimed he'd told her all there was to tell, that once Daniel emerged from the water the possibilities became too chaotic and unpredictable to discuss.

Marla didn't tell anyone Daniel was coming back. For the most part, no one would even know who she was talking about—some apprentice, dead for over half a decade?—and she didn't want to let Ernesto know, in case things didn't work out. Who knew how trustworthy the Giggler was anyway?

About ten months after she took down the Belly Killer, Marla started hanging out by the bay in her spare time, usually very early in the morning, watching the water.

On the third day, as she sat on a low stone wall in the shadow of a nearby crane, Marla noticed a rippling disturbance in the water. She stood up, heart surging... and then a blonde head broke the water.

The Bay Witch said, "Why the sitting and the staring?"

Marla blinked. Talking to the Bay Witch was tricky. The way she related to the world, and other people, was profoundly strange, but she was old, and powerful, and on the council, even if she didn't do much there, so you had to be polite. "I'm just... looking for someone."

The Bay Witch nodded. "Since you're here, come into the water and work while you look. Yes?"

"Ah... what do you want me to do?" Punch squid? Free lobsters from cages? She had no idea what the Bay Witch did under the waves all day.

"Clean dirty things," the Bay Witch said. "I'll make you so you can breathe in the water. Okay?"

Marla touched the stag beetle pin at her throat. "What about my cloak?"

"It will drag if you swim wearing it," the Bay Witch said. "But we'll put it safe under a rock down deep okay? I'll make it not get wet."

"Um..." The Bay Witch was looking at her expectantly. And it wasn't like Marla was doing anything useful sitting here anyway. Cultivating goodwill among the powerful couldn't hurt, though who knew if the Bay Witch would even remember Marla's name? "Okay," Marla said. "I'll help."

It was dirty work, scooping up pollutants, sorting through the crap on the floor of the bay, and whispering little death spells at certain invasive species the Bay Witch vigorously despised. Policing an ecosystem wasn't Marla's idea of fun, but it took her mind off other things, and the Bay Witch was pleasant enough company, in that she never much bothered with conversation. The sushi they had at lunch was always impossibly fresh. There were upsides.

And it was nice to be down in the water, because if Daniel did come trudging along the seafloor, she'd be the first to see him.

After a long morning under the waves, about eleven months after the Giggler's prophecy about Daniel, Marla rode the elevator up to Sauvage's penthouse. "Hey boss!" she shouted. "Which skulls need cracking today?"

Sauvage didn't answer, though, because Sauvage was dead.

He lay on his back before the vast unlit fireplace, his front awash in old cold blood, flies buzzing in the vicinity of his eyes. There wasn't much stink, which meant his guts hadn't been perforated. He'd been hit in the heart, maybe? With all that blood, he must have been stabbed with a post-hole digger.

Marla reversed her cloak, and her hyped-up senses assured her the apartment was devoid of other sentient life—but she did a quick pass through the other rooms anyway, finding no other signs of mess or theft; not even Sauvage's magical texts or implements were disturbed. She returned to his body, pulsing with the undirected wish to do violence, and the voice of the cloak whispering her toward indiscriminate massacre, but she still hesitated to reverse the color back to white. In the first flash of seeing Sauvage dead, she'd been numbed by shock; now the cold intelligence of the cloak insulated her from feeling grief or dismay. Once she returned to herself fully, she would have to bear those emotions.

But that was better than going out and killing every living thing in the city (to begin with), so she whispered "Turn." And sank to her knees beside her dead friend, trying to retain some shred of objectivity as she surveyed his wounds.

No more father figures, Marla thought. *They just die on you. Nobody you can depend on except for yourself.*

Sauvage's heart was missing, was the main thing. A messy hole had been torn just left of center in his chest, and while Marla's anatomical knowledge was strictly of the practical and learned-on-the-job variety, she could tell the organ had been completely removed.

She leaned over him, looking for some sign of who might have done this—was it too much to hope for a muddy bootprint, a cigarette butt, or some personal possession a forensic magician could use to track down the murderer?

There was a knife, on the far side of Sauvage's body—*the* knife, his dagger of office, a shining length of razored steel with the hilt wrapped in black and red electrical tape. There were all sorts of stories about that knife, which had been held by every chief sorcerer in Felport's history, but most people seemed to agree that it could cut through just about anything.

Sauvage, apparently, had used it to cut through some fingers, because there were a pair of severed digits on the floor next to it. *Good for you, boss.* The fingers were curiously grayish and withered, with long dirty fingernails, and she wrapped them in a bit of paper and stashed them in her shoulder bag. She looked at the knife for a moment, because the *other* widely agreed-upon story was that the dagger could defend itself, if anyone tried to take it from the owner without permission. Marla prodded the knife with a pencil, then reached out and tapped the hilt with her finger, and it just lay there, looking knifelike. Finally, knowing she had her cloak to save her if anything nasty happened, she closed her hand on the dagger's hilt.

It didn't bite her, shock her, or explode, so she figured, with its owner being dead, it was less picky about who handled it. She put the dagger away in her bag, too, carefully, where she wouldn't grab the blade by mistake. If she found the person who'd murdered Sauvage, she'd use the blade to dispatch them. Just a little poetry.

Marla fished out her cell phone to call Hamil. He was Sauvage's closest ally on the council, and a few months back, when Sauvage had spent a week vomiting ectoplasm after a botched séance, Hamil had stepped in to take over temporarily, though he hadn't needed to do much. Hamil was basically vice-president.

"Hamil," she said. "I've got bad news." She told him the situation, then took the elevator down to the basement.

The Giggler was snoring in a corner of his filthy little two-room suite under the water pipes, sitting cross-legged on a dirty blanket, his head resting against the damp brick wall. He wore only a pair of soiled underpants, and dandruff dusted his greasy black hair. Hard to believe he'd been the unstoppable terror of the sorcerous community less than a year ago.

Marla nudged him with her foot. He stirred, squinted, and smiled. "My savior. Feed me."

"In a minute. I have a question."

"I can tell the future," he said. "Or, maybe say, maybe say the future tells *me*. Things."

"I don't need to know the future. I need to know what happened to Sauvage."

The seer flinched at his master's name. "He met a challenger, but he didn't meet the challenge." He giggled. "I read the signs for him, the entrails and the water-spots, I told him no living hand would harm him."

Marla frowned. "You lied?"

He cringed away, hugging himself, and Marla smelled urine more strongly. The thought of lying to Sauvage made him wet himself in fear. "I don't lie. It's not my fault he asked the wrong questions."

"Okay," Marla said. "In that case, I have a question: What's the *right* question?"

"For you, for now? 'Where is the challenger'?"

Marla shook her head. "I've got his fingers. I'll be able to find him."

"Not this time. He can hide, easy, easy." The Giggler yawned. "So tired. Too many visions. Too many paths, so many end in fire and rubble and birdshit."

"Answer me. Where do I find the murderer?"

"Not murderer. Challenger."

"Find, where do I find him?"

"Feed me."

Marla sighed, took a few crumpled power bars from her bag, and tossed them into his lap. The Giggler devoured them, wrappers and all, then leaned back and closed his eyes. "You're up so high."

"What?"

"You climb among the ribs of the sky," he said dreamily, half a smile on his lips.

"Is that your answer?"

The Giggler belched.

"I could kill you, you know," she said.

"Shan't." He didn't open his eyes.

"Thanks," Marla said. "Helpful as always."

A block from Sauvage's building, as Marla cut through an alley, the birds attacked.

Mostly pigeons, but blackbirds, too, spiraling out of the sky like gray and black confetti. The birds blotted out the thin strip of sky and fell down on her, pecking and clawing and cawing and squawking. Finally, something to *hit*. She reversed her cloak and attacked them, but it was like trying to beat a feather mattress to death, like trying to dismember a cloud. The purple was nothing if not persistent, though, so she tore at the birds, her fingers sharp as razors, her teeth snapping at tiny feathered throats. The birds clutched at her cloak, hair, arms, and shoulders, trying to tear the cloak from her back.

No, worse—trying to carry *her* away. Her feet lifted an inch off the ground as the grasping birds tried to fly.

She snarled, her own mind a faraway observer seeing through a violet curtain. She fought under the weight of the birds, ripping them away and hurling them against the walls of the alley. She scissored her legs wildly, seeking purchase as she rose a foot, two feet, ten feet off the ground. This was ridiculous, impossible, it was cartoon physics, it was—

Well, magic, obviously. Would the birds take her to their master? Were they connected to Sauvage's death? Maybe, but they might just as easily peck out her eyes and drop her from a great height, so better to free herself. Besides, clothed in the purple, she wasn't capable of even strategic capitulation.

With considerable thrashing she managed to jostle the flock close to one side of the alley, where she hooked her feet under the edge of a stone window ledge. Having momentarily stopped her ascent, she opened her mouth to voice a spell—and a bird tried to shove itself down her throat.

She bit its body in half and spat out the remainder, then screamed "Incendia!"

The actual incarnation for calling down a storm of fire was rather more complex than a single word in Latin, but Sauvage had taught her a neat trick where she could spend the necessary fifteen minutes on the incantation in advance and create a single word to activate the spell at a later date—he called it "chanting a macro," and it saved a lot of time in life-or-death situations.

Marla fell to the floor of the alley, along with the charred and smoking remains of scores of birds. Sensing her grievous bodily harm—she wasn't fireproof, just because she'd called down the fire—her cloak reversed itself and began healing her wounds. She watched the surviving birds fly away, bumping into one another in their haste.

"Fucking birds," she said, once she could speak again. She sat up and spat blood and feathers out of her mouth. Who the hell in Felport ran a bird show these days? Even an alley witch could take control of a single pigeon, but to take a whole flock, make them work in concert, make them fight even in the face of certain death, and to do it all remotely? That took practice, specialization, and she didn't know any of the current sorcerers who could do that sort of thing, except maybe the idiot nature magician Granger, and he'd kill *himself* before letting harm come to one of his precious animals. There was nobody—

"Nobody alive," she said. What had the Giggler said about Sauvage? "No living hand would harm him." The severed fingers in her bag hadn't looked particularly healthy, even considering their disembodied state. And she could think of somebody who was *dead* who had a thing for using pigeons, and rats, and roaches, and other vermin to do his dirty work. Marla had heard stories about him. The chief sorcerer before Sauvage. A man who was brutal, ruthless, and universally feared. A man who, when he died, had been cut up into a dozen pieces, his parts scattered, just to forestall any conceivable resurrection.

The man Sauvage had challenged for leadership of the city, and defeated. The stories said, after he won, Sauvage tore open his enemy's chest, removed his heart, and devoured it to gain his strength. And earlier today someone had performed impromptu heart removal surgery on Sauvage himself. It was, at the very least, suggestive.

She opened her phone again. "Hamil," she said when he answered. "I think Somerset has come back from the dead." She looked at the dead birds around her feet and thought about the dagger of office in her bag. "And I'm pretty sure he wants his old job back."

Chapter Seventeen

"TEA?" HAMIL SAID, after Marla had rinsed feathers and bird blood out of her mouth at his kitchen sink.

"Sure. Anything to wash out the taste of Heckle and Jeckle."

Hamil busied himself with kettle and pots and cups while Marla sat at his granite kitchen counter—watching him make tea was like watching a bull do knitting, or an elephant building a ship in a bottle. "I'll call the council together," he said, "though I know Gregor is out of town—he's always off on some trip, he could benefit from spending more time close to home—and the Bay Witch can be difficult to reach. Messages in bottles are notoriously inefficient. I'm sure once they hear Somerset is alive… or, at least, conscious and mobile… they'll hurry."

"Great. While you guys are drafting an agenda, I'll just go find him and kill him—re-kill him. How about that?"

"Mmm. You and Sauvage were close. He spoke highly of you. Was there any, ah, compulsory…"

"A geas?" Marla shook her head. "No. I learned my lesson. Like George Washington said, no permanent treaties, no foreign entanglements. This is strictly a personal desire type thing. That, and he sent a flock of birds against me—though I don't know why he's picking on me, particularly."

Hamil poured a stream of pale brown liquid into a cup before her. "Because you have the knife, Marla. The dagger of office. Don't you?"

She started to blush, and scowled and ducked her head. "I was going to give it to you."

"No, keep it, for now. If you are planning to hunt Somerset, it will give you an edge. No pun intended."

"So he came after me to get the dagger? Why?"

"I assume he thinks you're planning to claim credit for his kill," Hamil said. "There have been occasional peaceful handovers of power in Felport's history, but not many. In theory, anyone can challenge the chief sorcerer to single combat, and take their place. That's how Sauvage took over from Somerset, though he had help from the city's other sorcerers, who assisted him in striking Somerset down."

Marla opened her mouth, closed it, opened it again: "Sauvage *cheated*?"

Hamil took a sip of tea. "Indeed. But cheating is allowed, of course. The point is to win, whatever the cost. If you can't defeat any challenger, the theory goes, then you don't deserve to be first among equals. Now, when Sauvage took over, he imposed a more democratic regime. The sorcerers vote on important matters, including who should be the next chief sorcerer. After Somerset's reign of terror, it was a welcome change, believe me. And it was a condition set by the other sorcerers when they agreed to help Sauvage kill the old king." He refilled his cup. "Because none of them could defeat Somerset alone. Not even Sauvage. As proven this morning, it seems."

"So Somerset thinks the old ways are still in force, and since I picked up the dagger, he thinks I'm trying to take his job?"

"Probably."

"Then why didn't *he* take the dagger?"

"Those severed fingers you showed me are the answer to that, Marla. The dagger isn't just a blade, it's an *artifact*, like your cloak—at least, on the same order. It is tied inextricably to the protection of Felport, and it would not have recognized a literally heartless undead monster like Somerset as an acceptable chief sorcerer. The dagger can protect itself, and when Somerset tried to pick it up after killing Sauvage, the dagger turned on him."

"Shit. So the most powerful sorcerer in the city's history is back from the dead, and he thinks I'm stepping on his territory. That's just grand."

"Mmm." Hamil took another sip. "It would be interesting to know how he came back to life. And where he is. Among other things."

"I've got a lead to follow up. I think I'll go do that."

"Would you like some assistance?"

"I work better alone," she said. "Thanks for the tea."

Marla walked to the half-finished Whitcroft-Ivory building, which would be the highest skyscraper in the city, if it ever got finished—it was currently slowly rusting, work abandoned in the midst of some property dispute.

You're so high, the Giggler had said—maybe the highest place in the city? Marla sat on a stack of weedy girders and considered the framework of the half-finished skyscraper. Dusk had arrived, the sun long gone behind the smokestacks to the west. Hundreds of birds circled counterclockwise over the building's jagged heights. *You climb among the ribs of the sky.*

The exposed girders might look like the ribs of the sky, she supposed, if you were half-mad and viewing them through a vision.

She began to climb, first on scaffolding, then jumping from one girder to the next, scaling up the metal poles when necessary. She took a break on the tenth floor, squinting up into the gloom. The birds still circled—a little faster now? She could have flown to the top, but she didn't want to miss any signs on the way. On the eighteenth floor she found a broad platform lashed to the girders above. A sorcerer's workspace? Some magic benefited from altitude, and while most magicians would choose a more accessible place for such work, Marla could believe a wizard waited above. Some magic benefited from desolation and things left unfinished, too.

She climbed a girder adjacent to the platform and found a man dressed in black lying face-down amid a mess of small bones, dried flowers, toppled blue bottles, and sticks of colored chalk. The birds circled placidly, not so far away now, making no move toward her. She jumped to the platform and turned the dead man over, recognizing him by his battered silk tophat and ridiculous white-skull facepaint. He was a necromancer named Upchurch. His chest had been messily opened, his heart removed, just like Sauvage's.

Marla had heard rumors about Upcurch lately, that he got drunk and bellowed about doing great magic, shouting secrets where even ordinaries could overhear. Now she found him up here with his works, wearing his ceremonial suit with the tiny silver skulls in place of buttons. "You dumb fucker," she whispered. "You found Somerset's body parts and raised him from the dead. Did you think he'd *thank* you?"

"You came." The voice emerged from the darkness off to the right, rattling like autumn leaves crushed underfoot.

Marla tensed, prepared to reverse her cloak, and threw out mental feelers. "Who's there?" she asked, though she knew.

"I am Somerset. Eclipse-bringer. Master of birds and rats and worms and vermin. Protector of Felport." A cold, earthy chuckle. "They may give me a new name now. They may call me Somerset, the Heartless."

"Nice to meet you," Marla said. "Heard a lot about you. Nothing good."

Somerset dropped from above—not even remotely from the direction his voice had come from. Nice trick.

At the sight of him, Marla thought of a mobile she'd once seen hanging in an occult bookstore, a rattling construction of shells and animal bones. Somerset was coathanger thin, spidery and strung-together, his skin pink and newly grown. His famous eyes left no doubt as to his identity: bright blue and flecked with orange, his irises rotated like slow pinwheels. Blood dripped from a gaping hole in his chest, and the ragged ends of ribs poked out into the cavity. He crouched like a gargoyle when he landed and licked his thin lips with a black tongue.

Even laying his crimes aside, Somerset was an abomination. You couldn't bring people back from the dead, not without dire consequences—they always brought the chill of death back with them, a sliver of darkness, their hand-me-down souls riddled with holes that could be invaded by terrible creatures with dark designs on the living. And to resurrect Somerset with no *heart*, his body not even complete... There was no chance he could be anything other than monstrous. She would destroy him so thoroughly that he could never be repaired.

Revolted, Marla reversed her cloak.

Her mind dissolved into cold rage, but before she could strike, Somerset lashed out with a hand fast as lightning and tore the stag-beetle-shaped cloak pin from her throat. He—he—how could he possibly move faster than her? It was *unreal*.

Her ferocity vanished as the cloak fell from her shoulders to the platform. The jolt of the artifact's sudden removal made her stagger and fall to her knees. Marla reached for the cloth, her natural reflexes now pitifully slow, but Somerset whipped one long leg past her and clutched the cloak with his toes, drawing it to him.

"Bad girl." He draped the cloak over his arm. "We need to speak. If you're obedient, you can have your toy back."

Though far from helpless without her cloak, Marla doubted she could beat him without it, not under these conditions. "I'm listening."

"This man revived me." Somerset gestured at Upchurch's body, then touched the edge of his empty heartspace. "A fierce hunger overcome me upon waking, and I tore open his chest, eager to eat his heart. My hunger was sated, and my wound closed.... but not for long. Soon, it opened again."

He's a ghoul, Marla thought, *a vampire, something from an old story.* She strained to keep her face composed. Eating hearts to survive... It was worse than she'd imagined. "So you killed Sauvage and ate his heart too."

"He ate mine first," Somerset said querulously.

"True, but how did you know? I mean, you were dead when it happened, so…"

"The dead know things, Marla." He smiled, his teeth smeared with blood and flecked with muscle tissue. "I thought if I ate Sauvage's heart it might restore me to my natural state, balance the scales." He looked away from Marla, out into the city, absently stroking her cloak with knobby fingers. "His heart gave me strength, but did not heal me. I also wanted to regain the dagger and my old position as chief of chiefs. Sauvage could not refuse my challenge. Nor could he defeat me."

Somerset's spinning eyes moved in perfect synchronicity with the wheeling birds above. She looked away from his face, blinking. Getting hypnotized now would not increase her likelihood of survival.

"You have my dagger," he said. "I watched you take it."

"Why didn't you take it yourself?" Knowing perfectly well, but stalling for time. Marla shivered in a gust of wind. The night was too cold to go without a cloak. She thought of snatching it away while he seemed distracted by the city below, but she doubted he was as distracted as he looked.

"I'm dead," Somerset said. "A monster." He held up his hand, two fingers missing, the ends raw but bloodless. "The dagger refused me. A dead thing cannot be the city's guardian. Understandable, but regrettable. I imagine most dead things lack my unique qualifications."

"So how about I hold onto the knife."

"My plan exactly. I sent my birds to bring you here, but you resisted. I'm glad you came on your own. Some seer guided you, I assume?"

"I've got all kinds of resources. Now I'm here—what do you want?" She thought she knew. She didn't think he'd accept a polite refusal, either.

"Be my puppet. You aren't fit to rule, a woman like you, coarse and uncouth, but I can stand behind you. You're just strong enough to be a convincing figurehead. You'll rule in name, but I'll rule in fact." He glanced down at her and sniffed. "You'll be well compensated, of course."

She shook her head. "You ran everything in the city personally, Somerset, and that's not how we do it anymore. There's a real sorcerers' council. They take *votes*."

"I've come back to stop that kind of nonsense. Accept my proposal."

"It's not nonsense. It's progress."

"You refuse me? I don't think you understand. Either agree to be my creature, or I will eat your heart. I can always force the other sorcerers to accept me as their ruler, dagger or no—I was merely hoping to ease the way, and avoid having to massacre the city's magic-users."

"This is the part where I say 'fuck you.'" Marla couldn't beat him without her cloak, but she could get away. She stepped backward off the platform, and Somerset screeched above her.

Falling, Marla focused all her will and wrenched space, taking the monumental and usually unnecessary risk of teleporting. Half the time she did this she got migraines—the kind so bad they make you puke—and there were *things* dwelling in between the dimensions, things that would grab you and tear you apart if they could. Spectral claws brushed her back, and something drew a searing line of pain across her thigh, but she emerged alive and whole in a dark basement beneath a ruined building, one of her dependable boltholes.

The migraine hit with a coruscation of flashing lights, and she sagged against the wall and shivered in the dark with pain.

"Somerset is in Sauvage's penthouse, wearing your cloak, demanding we pay allegiance to him, or die," Hamil said, once Marla dragged herself back to his apartment.

"Yeah?" Marla rubbed her temples. Her migraine had retreated to a dull throb. "What, is he on teleconference?"

"The magical equivalent," Hamil said. "Oh, and he wants us to bring you to him for execution." He yawned; it was well after midnight.

"Okay," Marla said. "Here's what you do. First, get Langford. I need something from him. Then tell Somerset okay, he can be chief sorcerer."

"Your plan is elegant in its incomprehensibility," he said.

"Because you haven't heard part three," Marla said, and explained.

"You'll probably die," Hamil said thoughtfully.

"Risk I have to take. Somerset killed my friend, which was bad enough, but then he took something that *belongs* to me."

"I didn't think you'd come," Marla said, lounging against an air-conditioning unit on the roof of Sauvage's building. A clear cold night, and the moon was a pretty stone high in the sky.

"Of course I came." Somerset scuttled forward, her cloak flapping from his shoulders, held closed with the pin Daniel had given her. For that alone she'd see him dead. Re-dead. Whatever. She noticed his fingers had grown back. The cloak was good, though not good enough to grow him a new heart, apparently. Too bad. It might have mellowed him.

"Mere moments after I am acknowledged as chief sorcerer, you dare challenge me for my position?" Somerset shook his head. "I would call it courage were it not madness. I even have your cloak."

"Yeah, about that. I want it back." She took the dagger of office from a sheath at her belt, considered the blade, and grinned at Somerset. "I think it goes really nicely with this knife. Accessories are very important for us modern women on the go."

"You will be dead before you—" he began, but didn't get much farther, because Marla said "Fuego" and hurled a fireball at his face.

Somerset threw himself backward to avoid the fireball, but Marla didn't let up. She'd been dosed with mongoose blood to speed her reflexes, and her fingernails were dripping blue-ringed octopus venom, and, mostly, she was really pissed at this asshole. She tossed a ball of tangled paperclips at Somerset, and they blossomed into razor spikes in midair, lashing toward him. He batted them away, losing a few more fingers in the process, but her cloak began healing him right away.

Birds started circling in the sky above, and Marla snapped her fingers and said "Zap," triggering the lightning-stones she'd secreted around the roof earlier. A net of lancing electricity arced above them, and the birds fell twitching like meaty hailstones before they could so much as crap on Marla.

She got close enough to kick Somerset in the face with her inertia-enchanted boot, and he snarled at her around broken teeth, grabbing her ankle and flinging her across the roof to bounce off a metal pole of uncertain utility. *Good thing I chewed those painkillers,* she thought, bouncing to her feet and coming at him again. She slashed at his eyes with her venomous claws, but he bent her wrist back, breaking it, and a pulse of that pain *did* get through, making her hiss. While he had his hand on her, though, she pulled her dagger and aimed at his guts, the preternaturally sharp blade slicing easily through his gray flesh...

But though it probably caused him pain, it didn't slow him down. The cloak healed him, and anyway, he was *dead.* The point wasn't to defeat him with punches, though. The point was to enrage him enough that he'd reverse the cloak, and for some reason he *wouldn't—*

"You dumb son of a bitch," she said, trying to press her knife into his throat with her one good hand. "You don't even know how to use the cloak, do you? Gods, I thought this would be a challenge. The secret word is 'turn,' you moron, just say *'turn'.*"

"Bitch," he snarled, shoving her off him. "I don't need any cloak to—"

She lashed out and sliced off one of his hands with the dagger. It really was an impressive weapon. He gasped and clutched the bloodless stump to his chest. "That'll take a while to grow back. And I notice the cloak isn't doing shit about that big gaping hole in your chest. Speaking of..." She reached into the pouch at her belt and lifted out a red cat's eye marble. "I'm going to stick this in your chest cavity. And guess what it's going to do? It's going to *explode*."

His eyes pinwheeled faster. He snarled.

He said "Turn."

Marla instantly sprinted for the edge of the building, but even so, she almost wasn't fast enough. Being inside the cloak was awesome, but being outside sucked. She saw only the barest glimpse of a shadowy purple blur in her peripheral vision as she turned. Those shadowy claws touched her back as she cleared the ledge and plummeted off the edge of the tall building. Somerset—lost in the cold, overconfident, single-minded murderousness of the cloak—came after her without hesitation.

Marla teleported again, reappearing instantly on the sidewalk below, this time without even a whisper of a headache, and unmolested by the things that dwelt in-between.

A moment later, small pieces of Somerset pattered down on the sidewalk all around her, much like the birds had fallen before. The cloak drifted down like a feather, unharmed, and she caught it out of the air. The stag beetle pin was still attached, and she draped the garment over her shoulders.

Hamil and Langford strolled out of the shadows. The biomancer looked up into the air alongside the building, where bits of Somerset still hung, seemingly floating in thin air. "A web of nanotube monofilament wires," he said. "Thin unto invisibility, sharper than a diamond edge, and when Somerset hit the wires..."

"Like putting him through a cheese grater," Marla said. "The cloak can't heal you when you get cut into several dozen pieces simultaneously."

"Not a use I would have considered for my monofilament technology," Langford said, "But sufficient to the task." He sighed. "I suppose I'm responsible for retrieving the wire?"

"Probably not a good idea to leave it up there," Marla said. "And you oughta pick up the bits and pieces of Somerset and dispose of them. I know they won't burn or dissolve in acid or anything—he's too packed with magic for that—but can't you put them in concrete and dump them in the ocean or something?"

"I suppose," Langford said. "We don't want another necromancer repeating Upchurch's experiment."

Marla stretched out her arms, though the cloak had already cured all her injuries, even her stiff muscles. Strolling along the sidewalk, she knelt and picked up what was left of the top of Somerset's head, the pinwheeling eyes turning slowly, slowly, slower, stopped.

"You did it," Hamil said.

"Yep. Is that sorcerer's council together yet?"

"They should be waiting at my apartment by now, awaiting your report," he said.

"Great." She put the top of Somerset's head into a plastic bag. "Let's go then."

"I'll need the dagger of office back."

"For now," Marla said, and handed it over.

When the sorcerers were assembled in Hamil's living room, Marla lifted out Somerset's head and said, "Looks like I solved your little vermin problem."

"We are most grateful," Susan Wellstone said. "We'll see you're compensated."

"Yep, you will," she said. "By making me the new chief sorcerer."

Gregor snorted. "That's nonsense. You're a... a *thug*."

"You guys told Somerset he was the boss. I challenged him to single combat, and won. By the old rules, that makes *me* the boss."

"The old rules aren't in effect anymore," Viscarro said. Something about him reminded Marla of Somerset, and not in a good way. "We're a democracy now."

"Sure. And if duly elected, I'll keep it that way. I'm all for progress. But for now I'm declaring my interest. Consider this my stump speech." She pointed to Somerset's head. "This is the stump."

"You don't even have standing to address this council, you're a freelance—" Susan Wellstone began, but Hamil cleared his throat.

"Actually, Susan," he said. "She wasn't freelance. She's been working for Sauvage for a year. And I happen to know he was grooming her for just this position. He didn't expect her time to come so soon, true, but nevertheless..." He shrugged. "I support her."

"Why do you believe yourself to be qualified?" the Chamberlain said, all cool elegance.

Marla brandished Somerset's head. "The gig is protector of Felport. See this guy? He threatened Felport. I protected the city against him. I'd say my case pretty much makes itself."

"There's more to this than brute force!" Gregor said, clenching the arms of his chair so hard his fingers went white. "It takes finesse, it takes skill, diplomacy, all qualities you lack!"

"That's why there's a council," Marla said. "You guys can advise me on that other stuff. Hamil says he'll be my consigliere."

"I had intended to put myself forward as successor—" Susan said, but Hamil cut her off again.

"We are addressing a different matter now, Susan. Time enough for your proposal if Marla's fails."

"Of course it will fail," Gregor said. "You can't possibly—"

"Our policies require a period of contemplation, reflection, and discussion before such a momentous decision," Hamil said. His position as chief sorcerer pro-tempore gave him permission to interrupt everybody, Marla figured. "We will reconvene in three days' time, at midnight, in Marla's presence, and take a vote on her proposal then." He turned to Marla, and the affable giant was gone; now he was chief sorcerer, no whiff of pro-tem about it. "And *you*, Marla. In the past day or so you've seen the corpses of the city's last two chief sorcerers dead at your feet. Take this time to meditate over whether this is a responsibility you truly want to bear."

"You guys take care," Marla said, tossing Somerset's head onto the floor before them. "And remember what I did for you tonight."

Ernesto, who hadn't said a word during the meeting, caught her eye and winked.

She grinned at him and walked out, feeling on top of the world. *No more father figures*, she thought. *It's about time I put myself in charge.*

When she approached her building, someone stepped out of the shadows next to her door. *Somerset*, she thought, in a moment of unreasoning terror, but then he stepped into the glow of a streetlight, and though he was thin, his clothes tattered, and his eyes shadowed, his identity was unmistakable:

"Daniel," she said, and he stepped trembling into her outstretched arms.

Chapter Eighteen

"I'M TEMPTED TO JUST DRAG YOU TO BED," Marla said, "But can I interest you in a shower first?"

Daniel shuddered. "Water. Do you know how sick I am. Of water." His voice was a strange croak, his skin was pale as a pearl, his flesh was clammy, and he stank of seaweed and low tide... but he was still Daniel.

"*Hot* water, baby," she soothed. "That makes all the difference. And I'll be in there with you."

They sat on her futon—the same futon where they'd once made love—with Daniel wrapped in Marla's terrycloth robe, drinking hot lemon tea, and slowly nibbling some stale crackers that were all Marla had in the cupboard. "I'm ravenous," he said. "I'd tell you to order all the Chinese food in the world, but I'm afraid if I try to eat any faster than this, I'll puke it all up." He put his hand on her knee, and it didn't seem to weigh any more than a leaf. He was thinner than Marla remembered, but she supposed years at the bottom of the sea might do that to a person. "How long has it been?" he said. "For me, time, there was no time, except for the walking, and even then, I lost track. So..."

"Seven years. And about a year of that was spent walking here, I think."

"Seven..." he murmured. Then he smiled, and though it was watered-down and troubled, it was still a flash of the boy she'd loved. "Then we have a lot of catching up to do." He kissed her, tentatively, and she helped him out of his robe, and she was gentle. The first time.

The next morning—more properly early afternoon—she went out and got bagels and coffee, but almost ran on the way home for fear Daniel might… what? Disappear? Be driven by the geas to go kill immediately? Surely Artie's ghost, or the emotional recording that served that purpose, wasn't happy with the time they were spending on this reunion. But Daniel was there, sitting at her counter, listening to National Public Radio with a bemused look on his face. "*He's* president?" Daniel said.

"You know what they say: it's not who you are, it's who you know. Or who your daddy is, I guess," Marla said. "I brought food."

"Good. I want to eat. Subsisting on the life energy of a monstrous elder god might keep you alive, but it doesn't fill your belly." He sipped coffee, winced, and smiled. "Heat. I can't get used to heat. I think my core temperature is legally dead." He sighed. "Okay. So I know Artie's gone, because that's what woke me up, his voice in my ear. But… Jenny?"

Marla shook her head minutely. What could she say? "Jenny loved you, and so she torched herself when she thought you died?" She settled for, "She made it back, told us what happened, but we, ah, couldn't save her."

Daniel went paler than before, if that were possible, but finally just nodded. "Ernesto?"

"Oh, he's fine. Hell, he's on the sorcerer's council. Want to see him?"

"No," Daniel said quickly. "No, not like… not like this. Let me get myself put back together again. You, you're here, you're inside my heart, I don't mind if you see me like this, but nobody else. Wow. The council? Good for him."

"Oh, that's nothin'." Marla beamed at him. "There's a good chance that in two days' time I'll be named chief sorcerer."

Daniel just stared at her. "What. What do you mean?"

"My star is on the rise. I've performed great services to Felport, and the council's going to vote in a few days."

He put his hand to his forehead. "This… I don't know what to say. You have to understand, for me, it's like I just saw you a few weeks ago, maybe months, my head is so scrambled, it's so loud… How can you be chief sorcerer? We're just apprentices."

Marla bristled, and tried to stop herself from bristling. "Well, no. You've been asleep, I guess, but I've been busting my ass, getting to know people—I was Sauvage's right hand until he died."

"Sauvage is dead? But he was so…" Daniel made a vague gesture, then shook his head. "This is too much, Marla. I can't… I need some air. Can we go out? Somewhere high? Somewhere way the hell up above sea level?"

"My roof is awesome," Marla said, though in truth, she hadn't spent much time there, since Jenny immolated herself.

They sat on the roof, a cool breeze blowing by, and Daniel was silent; dour, even. Finally Marla said, "So what happened to you?"

Daniel shrugged, staring off at the towers of the financial district in the distance. "Jenny told you most of the story, right? When I was trying to swim out, one of the god's tentacles, filaments, whatever, grabbed me. It pulled me down, and there were... not even mouths. Like, vents. Gills. But they were lined with teeth. It wanted to eat me. But it was touching me, so..." He shrugged. "Sucking out life force is always easier when there's direct contact, so I tried to drain its life. But it was like drinking from a firehose. Just torrents of power flowing into me. Must have hurt the god a little, though, because it flung me away, down, and I don't know if it was because its life energy was so strange, or if it was because I was injured, or if I was too deep in the water for my brain to cope with the pressure, or what, but everything went dark. I thought I was dying, but I guess not. All that god-energy must have sustained me while I hibernated. Or whatever." He gave Marla a little smile. "I dreamed, though. I dreamed of you.

"I woke up with Artie yammering in my ear that he was dead and I better come fulfill my obligations, so I swam, and walked on the bottom of the sea, and swam some more. It was dark, cold, miserable, and I burned off whatever remained of the god-energy fast. I lived off the life energy of fish and sharks and plankton and stuff for most of the walk. And now... here I am. But I feel like a guy who's been in a coma. The world's passed me by."

"Don't say that," Marla said. "I'm here. I'm still here for you. I mean, you can work for me. Even if they don't make me chief sorcerer, I'm still a person of consequence now, they'll probably throw me a seat on the council at the very least, you can..." She trailed off, because Daniel didn't even seem to be listening, just stared, faraway. Marla tried to imagine what it must be like for him, going through all that, and coming back. She wasn't sure she possessed that level of empathy.

Finally she said, "The geas must be bothering you. If you want to, we can go kill the guy, and get Artie off your back."

Daniel turned his head to her slowly, frowning. "Kill... kill who?"

"The guy who murdered Artie."

"You haven't killed him yet? But... what? How?"

"It's a long story. My geas was broken. But—you must have known the murderer was still alive, I mean, if I'd killed him, you wouldn't be here, right?"

"Marla. My geas wasn't about avenging Artie."

"What do you mean?"

"Artie wanted to be immortal more than anything," Daniel said. "My geas is to bring Artie back to *life*."

"No fucking way. I just killed one back-from-the-dead abomination *yesterday*. You're not... you can't... are you *crazy*? He's been in the ground for a year, there's no way—"

"It's trivial," Daniel said. "We dig up his body. I fill him with life-force. It might not be Artie exactly like he was, but it'll have his mind, his memories, his powers—"

"Daniel, baby, you aren't listening. I can't allow this. Bringing people back from the dead... they become monsters. They bring back fragments of Hell."

He shrugged, not even interested in the discussion. "What can I tell you? It's the geas. It's not optional. Where's he buried?"

"Baby. No."

He stood up, staring down at her, and he was suddenly the petulant boy she'd first met, the one so quick to anger and take offense, the one who thought he knew more and better than anyone else. "You don't get to tell me no. You're not *my* chief sorcerer, gods, as if that's even... as if you could... You didn't even do your part, you didn't even avenge Artie? I have to bring him back to a world where his killer still walks around? Who are you? What are you? We were family."

"I'm what we dreamed of being, Daniel," she said, rising herself. "Successful, strong, powerful. And if this *is* going to be my city, I can't have the resurrected body of Artie Mann lurching through it like some kind of half-assed zombie demanding cigars instead of brains—"

He flinched back. "Artie saved you. He picked you up when you were just a piece of trash on the street, he—he's the reason you have anything! And you want to make a mockery of our promises to him, of our *family*? What's wrong with you?"

"Okay, yes, that wasn't cool, I'm sorry, but there are things we can do, ways we can try to break the geas on you..."

"I don't want to break it!" he screamed. He stormed across the roof, as far away from her as he could, all the way to the edge. "I want to fulfill my promises! That promise to Artie is the only reason I'm standing here! You, you left me on the bottom of the sea, you left me for dead, and it didn't slow you down at all, didn't even put a dent in your momentum, Miss chief-fucking-sorcerer! And now you want to stop me? No. No, I'm going to raise Artie, right now, I can find him, I can find the heat signature of the end of his life and—"

"You can't." Marla approached him, slowly, like he was a feral cat, thinking, *Gods, he was in the ocean for a year, getting nibbled by fish, he's probably half crazy.* "We can get you help, Daniel, you'll see, you'll understand." She put her hand on his shoulder.

And he began stealing her life.

She gasped and fell to her knees, but she was wearing her cloak, as always, and it fought him, kept her from dying, and she knew without it, she'd be dead already—he was *draining* her.

"Betrayed me," he snarled, "abandoned me, don't you understand, Artie is howling in MY HEAD, he's been screaming at me for a year, and you, you just *got over it*, you just broke your *promises*, you—"

The cloak couldn't keep up. Daniel was getting healthier before her eyes, his cheeks flushing with color, and she thought, *He doesn't know what he's doing*, thought about the way he'd stolen the life from his sister, thought about death, her impending death, how she might die, and Daniel might raise Artie, and there would be another monster... here... in her city.

Blackness began to shimmer before her eyes, and some deep self-preservation instinct kicked in, and the word whispered in her mind was: *TURN.*

She was cloaked in the purple. She took Daniel by the arms. She twisted her hips.

She threw Daniel off the roof. And he fell.

It took him two days to die. She brought his broken but breathing body to her apartment, and draped the cloak over him, and waited for its healing work to begin. She stayed by his side, and wept over him, and begged his forgiveness, and offered to bring Artie's corpse and lay it at his feet, to help him do whatever he needed to do. The cloak made his body knit together, but he didn't open his eyes, not until early in the morning on the second day.

"I'm going to die," he said.

"No, Daniel, you can be healed, it's—"

"I want to." His voice a murmur, almost affectless. "I tried to hurt you. To kill you. I made you kill *me*."

"Daniel—"

"I just want it to be black and dark again. I just want to go back to sleep forever and dream of you. The way you used to be. The way we used to be." She could almost see the life leaving him, see him pushing it out of himself, opening a hole to let all the life drain out. Daniel closed his eyes.

He didn't open them again.

Marla couldn't stop shaking. Hamil was rubbing her shoulders, speaking in a soothing voice, saying, "We'll see he's given a good burial," saying, "It's a terrible loss, I'm so sorry," saying all the empty things you say.

"I killed him," she croaked at last, and stared down into the cup of tea he'd set before her at some point. The liquid was cold now.

"From what you said—what I was able to piece together from what you said—he let himself die. He chose it."

"I threw him. Off a roof. He's dead. It's my fault."

"Marla," he said after a moment. "You know the vote is tonight, but it's clear, you're in no state… Would you like to withdraw your name from consideration? No one will think less of you. If there's one thing sorcerers understand, it's tragedy."

She looked at Hamil, at his concerned face, another big man who was willing to let her lean on him, another man who was willing to take the weight and help her, and she ground her teeth together. "No," she said. "I want to be chief sorcerer. I deserve it." *And I have nothing else left.*

"Marla, you'll have to meet with the other sorcerers tonight, present yourself for the vote, and they'll be able to sense your… distress, your distraction, and the vote is already too close to call, I suspect. There's no way—"

"Forget-me-lots," she said suddenly.

He frowned. "What?"

"The potion we use when ordinaries see something they shouldn't, to wipe out their memories of whatever they witnessed, and mold new harmless memories to fill in the gaps. Yes. Do that to me. Make me forget… what happened to Daniel."

"What you're asking, it's not temporary, Marla, you understand? I can't make you forget just for tonight, and—"

"That's fine. Forever. Take it all away forever. I don't want the grief. I don't want the weakness. The past…" She slammed her hand down on the table hard, making the cup rattle and slosh. "Fuck the past. What did love ever do for me except make me weak? Take it all. Slice Daniel right out of my head." She was expressing anger to cover the black hole opening up inside her. She'd had Daniel; lost him; regained him… thrown him off a fucking *building*. He'd preferred to die rather than adjust to a new life with her. He'd called her a traitor. Her mind could go nowhere except to Daniel.

"This isn't a decision to make in haste, Marla. Our experiences shape us, make us who we are. A man died. You shouldn't just forget that. It—"

"So let me remember the killing, just not… who it was. Hamil. I don't have time to think and reflect. This is my chance to achieve what I've dreamed of. To have a real purpose. I'll dedicate my life to Felport, but this… you have to help me clear my *head*."

After a long moment he said, "It will have to be lethe water. Forget-me-lots isn't potent enough for the kind of forgetting you want."

"Fine, bring out the high-test, whatever, let's just do it."

"Who knows about your relationship with Daniel?"

"Nobody alive, except Ernesto. And he never mentions him to me. He knows it's a sore point. And I'm the only one who knows Daniel came back, except for you. Everyone thinks he's dead. Let him stay dead."

"All right," Hamil said. "If you really want this, I'll call Langford."

"I really want it." *Because it's either forget, or be a failure, and hate myself, and die, and I'm not ready to die.*

Marla yawned and sat up on the exam table, Langford and Hamil peering at her. "So, doc, did I check out? Am I physically fit to be Felport's big boss?"

"You seem to be in working order," Langford said. "We just need to test your mental acuity."

"Shoot." She was jazzed, full of adrenaline and energy, ready to stand before the council and convince any of them that needed convincing.

"Tell me," Langford said, "Did you kill a man this week?"

Marla stiffened. "Shit. I guess I should have known word would get around. It was just, it was stupid, we were tussling over this stupid magical item, some enchanted deck of cards wrapped in silk. I was working for some guy in the Honeyed Knots, the other guy was working for who knows who, and… things got out of hand. He fell off the roof."

"Fell?" Hamil said.

She shrugged. "Okay, so I pushed. I didn't mean to kill him, but I take responsibility. I guess I should visit his grave. Leave flowers or something."

"I'll find out where he's buried," Hamil said. "Tell me, do you remember a boy named Daniel?'

No bells rang whatsoever. "Huh. Can you give me some context? Sort of a generic name."

"He knew Artie Mann…"

Marla snapped her fingers. "Right! He was one of Artie's apprentices, wasn't he? Didn't he die out in the field, like, ten years ago?"

"Closer to seven," Hamil said.

Marla shrugged. "I didn't know him that well. I think Jenny said she had a crush on him." She looked at the ceiling for a moment. "Gods, Ernesto and me are the only ones who made it out of Artie's world alive, aren't we?"

"One last question, Marla," Hamil said. "Have you ever been in love?"

"Ha. Love? I love three things: this city, punching people, and I forget the third thing."

"All right, then," Hamil said. "Shall we go see the council?"

Marla was annoyed. She didn't get to make an opening statement or anything. She just had to sit there while Hamil took the vote.

"I call the question," Hamil said. "Do we accept Marla Mason as our new chief sorcerer, first among equals and protector of Felport?"

Almost everyone was there, arrayed in a semi-circle with Marla seated in the center, doing her best to look cool and worthy of command. Viscarro had refused to come out of his catacombs again, but he was on speakerphone. Even Granger and the Bay Witch were there, and they habitually abstained from *everything*, being perfectly obsessed with their domains of park and water to the exclusion of most everything else.

"I vote yes," Hamil said.

"No," the Chamberlain said.

"No," Susan Wellstone said.

"No," Gregor said.

This isn't going too well, Marla thought.

"I vote yes," Viscarro said, and Susan gasped, and Gregor shouted, "What?"

"I owe no explanation," Viscarro's tinny voice said. "But I will offer one. Miss Mason, I believe you will be a weak and ineffectual chief sorcerer, and that with you in charge, I will be able to do whatever I wish without fear of effective interference."

"You know I'm going to remember you said that," Marla said.

"I do," Viscarro replied. "But the point is I think you're going to be useless, so I don't *care*."

"The vote stands," Hamil said mildly. "Motivation is irrelevant."

"I vote yes, too," Ernesto said.

"Fine," Susan said. "Then it's a tie—three votes for Marla, three against. And, as our bylaws state, tie goes to the status-quo. Marla's candidacy fails—"

"I didn't vote yet," Granger said, looking up from the careful examination of something he'd found in his nose.

"And how do you vote?" Hamil said.

"I abstain," he said, and looked back down.

"Yes, well, since *that's* done," Susan said.

"I vote yes," the Bay Witch said. She stepped over to Marla and kissed her on both cheeks very solemnly, leaving briny wet spots, and said, "Congratulations, new boss lady."

"But you *always* abstain!" Gregor said, aghast.

"Not always. Marla. Thank you for helping me clean up the bay."

"Oh, I see, currying favor," Susan said, "sucking up to one of us to secure her vote, that's just—"

"Just the sort of diplomacy and alliance-building you believed Marla incapable of achieving," Hamil said. "Be gracious, Susan. The motion passes. Marla Mason is our new chief sorcerer."

Marla cleared her throat. She hadn't helped clean up the bay to curry favor, she'd done it because—because—

It was like there was a sudden drop-off in her mind, deep dark water with no bottom in sight. Well, who cared why. *Maybe I'm just smarter than I thought.* "Thank you for this opportunity. I love this city. I'll do everything in my power to defend it, and to ensure the prosperity of everyone in this room." She paused. "Even you assholes who voted against me."

"This opens what is sure to be a very interesting era in the history of Felport," Hamil said. "Your dagger, Marla." He passed her the dagger of office, the hilt now wrapped in bands of purple and white electrical tape. Not the ceremonial colors she'd have chosen, but she couldn't say they were inappropriate.

Gregor and Susan stormed off in a huff, Granger wandered vaguely away, Ernesto shook her hand vigorously and grinned, and the Chamberlain murmured something surprisingly gracious on her way out. Viscarro just hung up his phone without comment.

The Bay Witch paused at Marla's side. "I saw a boy in the water a few days ago."

"Um… okay?" Marla said. She was grateful to the woman, but the Bay Witch was *odd*.

"A little fish told me that boy is dead. I'm sorry for your loss."

"I'm sorry, too?"

The Bay Witch nodded seriously and departed.

Hamil smiled. "Well, Marla. Will you be taking over Sauvage's penthouse?"

"I don't think so. I've been pretty friendly with Rondeau this past year, I think maybe I'll set up shop in the empty office space above his club, you know? The shit I put that kid through, paying him some rent is the least I can do."

"I do support you making amends with him however you can," Hamil said. "It's important to learn from our mistakes."

"Better to never make mistakes in the first place." Marla grinned.

"Mmm. Do you think so? I wonder. Would you like a celebratory drink?"

"Why the hell not. I'm on top of the world."

While Hamil went to the bar, Marla walked out on his balcony, and looked down on the city, *her* city. *From nothing,* she thought. *What was it Artie used to say? Magic is a foul rag and bone shop. Maybe so. But this is a foul rags to fabulous riches story if I ever heard one.*

Hamil handed her a glass of bourbon and joined her at the railing. "To fallen friends," he said, raising his glass.

"To the future," Marla countered, and after a strangely long moment—what was that about?—Hamil nodded, and clinked his glass against hers.

■

Acknowledgments

I'D LIKE TO THANK EVERYONE who donated when this book was an online serial—I'd list all the names, but it would take pages, and some of them may wish to be anonymous, so I'll err on the side of discretion. Thanks also to everyone who blogged, tweeted, or otherwise told their friends about Bone Shop. Spreading the word is the most important thing, and I had ample help.

I usually thank all my first readers, but since I had to post a new chapter every week (sometimes only writing it the night before!), my only first reader was my wife, Heather Shaw, who was a tireless cheerleader. I couldn't have done it without her.

Thanks to Tiffany Baxendell Bridge for e-book assistance; to Mur Lafferty for assorted advice; to Jeremy Tolbert for technical suggestions; to Marla superfan Shannon Johnson for various forms of assistance; and to Anne Rodman for encouraging me to write about the origins of Marla Mason.

www.ingramcontent.com/pod-product-compliance
Lightning Source LLC
Chambersburg PA
CBHW072125170626
46813CB00004B/1699